OLD MOTHER WEST WIND

The Centennial Anniversary Edition

OLD MOTHER WEST WIND

The Centennial Anniversary Edition

THORNTON W. BURGESS

With Illustrations by George Kerr

PUBLISHED IN ASSOCIATION WITH THE
THORNTON W. BURGESS MUSEUM AND THE
GREEN BRIAR NATURE CENTER, SANDWICH, MASSACHUSETTS,
BY
DOVER PUBLICATIONS, INC., MINEOLA, NEW YORK

Bibliographical Note

This Dover edition, first published in 2011 in association with the Thornton W. Burgess Museum and the Green Briar Nature Center, Sandwich, Massachusetts, who have provided a new Foreword, is an unabridged republication of the following two books: *Old Mother West Wind,* originally published by Little, Brown, and Company, Boston, in 1910 and *Mother West Wind's Children,* originally published by Little, Brown, and Company, Boston, in 1911. All of the original George Kerr illustrations have been included.

Library of Congress Cataloging-in-Publication Data

Burgess, Thornton W. (Thornton Waldo), 1874–1965.
    Old Mother West Wind : the centennial anniversary edition / Thornton W. Burgess ; with illustrations by George Kerr.
        p. cm.
    "This Dover edition . . . is an unabridged republication of the following two books: Old Mother West Wind, originally published by Little, Brown, and Company, Boston, in 1910 and Mother West Wind's Children, originally published by Little, Brown, and Company, Boston, in 1911"—Copyright p.
    Summary: The adventures of Peter Rabbit, Johnny Chuck, Reddy Fox, the Merry Little Breezes, and all their companions in the fields, the woods, and the streams.
    ISBN-13: 978-0-486-48051-0
    ISBN-10: 0-486-48051-8
        1. Children's stories, American. 2. Animals—Juvenile fiction. [1. Animals—Fiction.] I. Kerr, George, ill. II. Burgess, Thornton W. (Thornton Waldo), 1874–1965. Mother West Wind's children. III. Title. IV. Title: Mother West Wind's children.
PZ7.B917Om 2011
[Fic]—dc22

                                                                              2010045238

Manufactured in the United States by Courier Corporation
48051801
www.doverpublications.com

CONTENTS

Mother West Wind's Children (1911)

LIST OF ILLUSTRATIONS

FOREWORD

Welcome to the 100th Anniversary edition of *Old Mother West Wind,* the first children's book written by Thornton W. Burgess, one of the most widely read authors of the twentieth century. This edition also includes his second children's book, *Mother West Wind's Children.* At the time he wrote these books, Thornton was an editor at *Good Housekeeping.* Prior to that he had written some song lyrics, some advertising copy, and a book best forgotten, called *The Bride's Primer.*

Old Mother West Wind, like many children's classics, began with a child, at home. In 1909 Thornton Burgess began to make up stories for his son about the birds and animals of the ponds and woodlands based on his own observations while growing up in Sandwich, Massachusetts.

When business called him away from home, he would write letters back with new stories to be read to little Thornton. Old Mother West Wind and her children, the Merry Little Breezes, were the universal observers, helping to carry the narrative from one scene to another.

Eventually, Burgess collected these stories and sold them to the publishing house of Little, Brown, and Company of Boston. In 1910 they published the collection under the name *Old Mother West Wind.* This book introduced characters who were to continue for fifty years, through seventy full-length books, 100 mini-books, 15,000 syndicated newspaper "Bedtime Stories," and as-yet-uncounted magazine short stories. Burgess also read his stories and answered questions about bird and animal behavior on a radio show called, "The Radio Nature League" that he did for free during its ten-year run.

As if this were not enough to keep one man busy, Thornton Burgess also worked for conservation, often in conjunction with Dr. William Hornaday of the New York Zoological Society.

He first used the "Green Meadow Club" that he had originally conceived for children, as a vehicle to create bird sanctuaries across the country. Utilizing his syndicated columns in newspapers and magazines, he encouraged children to ask their parents and neighbors to set aside land where songbirds would be protected. By 1921, over two and a half million acres had been privately pledged as sanctuaries, largely due to his efforts.

In 1918 he joined the fight to pass the first Migratory Bird Act, designed to protect migratory waterfowl. It proposed what would be the first hunting season in the United States. Prior to that time, anyone could hunt anything in any quantity at any time. Burgess, never a fan of hunting for sport, wrote *The Adventures of Poor Mrs. Quack* to dramatize the plight of the birds. The bill passed, and a new era of conservation began.

Throughout his life he felt a responsibility to answer children's questions about nature. He knew they looked to him for answers and if he didn't know the answer himself, he would find it and reply to their correspondence. He was unusual for his time and almost unimaginable for ours.

Today, Dover Publications is helping to make more and more Burgess books available to the public every year. All are carefully reproduced from the original first editions. We at The Thornton W. Burgess Society in Sandwich are happy to help Dover carry out the commitment to quality in children's literature that this book epitomizes. We strive to preserve his memory and to carry on his commitment to Nature Education.

Together, we hope that you and your children (or grandchildren) will enjoy this 100th Anniversary edition of *Old Mother West Wind* as much as the generations that have gone before.

JOHN RICHMOND
Thornton W. Burgess Society

OLD MOTHER WEST WIND

by

THORNTON W. BURGESS

*To my Mother to whom I owe so much
and to my little son
whose love of stories inspired
these tales
this little volume is
affectionately dedicated.*

Johnny didn't stop to think that
Reddy Fox was twice as big as he. *Page 22.*

CHAPTER I

~

MRS. REDWING'S SPECKLED EGG

Old Mother West Wind came down from the Purple Hills in the golden light of the early morning. Over her shoulders was slung a bag—a great big bag—and in the bag were all of Old Mother West Wind's children, the Merry Little Breezes.

Old Mother West Wind came down from the Purple Hills to the Green Meadows and as she walked she crooned a song:

"Ships upon the ocean wait;
    I must hurry, hurry on!
Mills are idle if I'm late;
    I must hurry, hurry on."

When she reached the Green Meadows Old Mother West Wind opened her bag, turned it upside down and shook it. Out tumbled all the Merry Little Breezes and began to spin round and round for very joy, for you see they were to play in the Green Meadows all day long until Old Mother West Wind should come back at night and take them all to their home behind the Purple Hills.

First they raced over to see Johnny Chuck. They found Johnny Chuck sitting just outside his door eating his breakfast. One, for very mischief, snatched right out of Johnny Chuck's mouth the green leaf of corn he was eating, and ran away with it. Another playfully pulled his whiskers, while a third rumpled up his hair.

Johnny Chuck pretended to be very cross indeed, but really he didn't mind a bit, for Johnny Chuck loved the Merry Little Breezes and played with them every day.

And if they teased Johnny Chuck they were good to him, too. When they saw Farmer Brown coming across the Green Meadows with a gun one of them would dance over to Johnny Chuck and whisper to him that Farmer Brown was coming, and then Johnny Chuck would hide away, deep down in his snug little house under ground, and Farmer Brown would wonder and wonder why it was that he never, never could get near enough to shoot Johnny Chuck. But he never, never could.

When the Merry Little Breezes left Johnny Chuck they raced across the Green Meadows to the Smiling Pool to say good morning to Grandfather Frog, who sat on a big lily pad watching for green flies for breakfast.

"Chug-arum," said Grandfather Frog, which was his way of saying good morning.

Just then along came a fat green fly and up jumped Grandfather Frog. When he sat down again on the lily pad the fat green fly was nowhere to be seen, but Grandfather Frog looked very well satisfied indeed as he contentedly rubbed his white waistcoat with one hand.

"What is the news, Grandfather Frog?" cried the Merry Little Breezes.

"Mrs. Redwing has a new speckled egg in her nest in the bulrushes," said Grandfather Frog.

"We must see it," cried the Merry Little Breezes, and away they all ran to the swamp where the bulrushes grow.

Now someone else had heard of Mrs. Redwing's dear little nest in the bulrushes, and he had started out bright and early that morning to try and find it, for he wanted to steal the little speckled eggs just because they were pretty. It was Tommy Brown, the farmer's boy.

When the Merry Little Breezes reached the swamp where the bulrushes grow they found poor Mrs. Redwing in great distress. She was afraid that Tommy Brown would find her dear little nest, for he was very, very near it, and his eyes were very, very sharp.

"Oh," cried the Merry Little Breezes, "we must help Mrs. Redwing save her pretty speckled eggs from bad Tommy Brown!"

So one of the Merry Little Breezes whisked Tommy Brown's old straw hat off his head over into the Green Meadows. Of course Tommy ran after it. Just as he stooped to pick it up another little Breeze ran away with it. Then they took turns, first one little Breeze, then another little Breeze running away with the old straw hat just as Tommy Brown would almost get his hands on it. Down past the Smiling Pool and across the Laughing Brook they raced and chased the old straw hat, Tommy Brown running after it, very cross, very red in the face, and breathing very hard. Way across the Green Meadows they ran to the edge of the wood, where they hung the old straw hat in the middle of a thorn tree. By the time Tommy Brown had it once more on his head he had forgotten all about Mrs. Redwing and her dear little nest. Besides, he heard the breakfast horn blowing just then, so off he started for home up the Lone Little Path through the wood.

And all the Merry Little Breezes danced away across the Green Meadows to the swamp where the bulrushes grow to see the new speckled egg in the dear little nest where Mrs. Redwing was singing for joy. And while she sang the Merry Little Breezes danced among the bulrushes, for they knew, and Mrs. Redwing knew, that some day out of that pretty new speckled egg would come a wee baby Redwing.

CHAPTER II

~

WHY GRANDFATHER FROG HAS NO TAIL

Old Mother West Wind had gone to her day's work, leaving all the Merry Little Breezes to play in the Green Meadows. They had played tag and run races with the Bees and played hide and seek with the Sun Beams, and now they had gathered around the Smiling Pool where on a green lily pad sat Grandfather Frog.

Grandfather Frog was old, very old, indeed, and very, very wise. He wore a green coat and his voice was very deep. When Grandfather Frog spoke everybody listened very respectfully. Even Billy Mink treated Grandfather Frog with respect, for Billy Mink's father and his father's father could not remember when Grandfather Frog had not sat on the lily pad watching for green flies.

Down in the Smiling Pool were some of Grandfather Frog's great-great-great-great-great-grandchildren. You wouldn't have known that they were his grandchildren unless someone told you. They didn't look the least bit like Grandfather Frog. They were round and fat and had long tails and perhaps this is why they were called Pollywogs.

"Oh Grandfather Frog, tell us why you don't have a tail as you did when you were young," begged one of the Merry Little Breezes.

Grandfather Frog snapped up a foolish green fly and settled himself on his big lily pad, while all the Merry Little Breezes gathered round to listen.

"Once on a time," began Grandfather Frog, "the Frogs ruled the world, which was mostly water. There was very little dry land—oh, very little indeed! There were no boys to throw stones and no hungry Mink to gobble up foolish Frog-babies who were taking a sun bath!"

Billy Mink, who had joined the Merry Little Breezes and was listening, squirmed uneasily and looked away guiltily.

"In those days all the Frogs had tails, long handsome tails of which they were very, very proud indeed," continued Grandfather Frog. "The King of all the Frogs was twice as big as any other Frog, and his tail was three times as long. He was very proud, oh, very proud indeed of his long tail. He used to sit and admire it until he thought that there never had been and never could be another such tail. He used to wave it back and forth in the water, and every time he waved it all the other Frogs would cry 'Ah!' and 'Oh!' Every day the King grew more vain. He did nothing at all but eat and sleep and admire his tail.

"Now all the other Frogs did just as the King did, so pretty soon none of the Frogs were doing anything but sitting about eating, sleeping and admiring their own tails and the King's.

"Now you all know that people who do nothing worth while in this world are of no use and there is little room for them. So when Mother Nature saw how useless had become the Frog tribe she called the King Frog before her and she said:

"'Because you can think of nothing but your beautiful tail it shall be taken away from you. Because you do nothing but eat and sleep your mouth shall become wide like a door, and your eyes shall start forth from your head. You shall become bow-legged and ugly to look at, and all the world shall laugh at you.'

"The King Frog looked at his beautiful tail and already it seemed to have grown shorter. He looked again and it was shorter still. Every time he looked his tail had grown shorter and smaller. By and by when he looked there was nothing left but a little stub which he couldn't even wriggle. Then even that disappeared, his eyes popped out of his head and his mouth grew bigger and bigger."

Old Grandfather Frog stopped and looked sadly at a foolish green fly coming his way. "Chug-arum," said Grandfather Frog, opening his mouth very wide and hopping up in the air. When he sat down again on his big lily pad the green fly was nowhere to be seen. Grandfather Frog smacked his lips and continued:

"And from that day to this every Frog has started life with a big tail, and as he has grown bigger and bigger his tail has grown smaller and smaller, until finally it disappears, and then he remembers how foolish and useless it is to be vain of what nature has given us. And that is how I came to lose my tail," finished Grandfather Frog.

"Thank you," shouted all the Merry Little Breezes. "We won't forget."

Then they ran a race to see who could reach Johnny Chuck's home first and tell him that Farmer Brown was coming down on the Green Meadows with a gun.

CHAPTER III

~

HOW REDDY FOX WAS SURPRISED

Johnny Chuck and Reddy Fox lived very near together on the edge of the Green Meadows. Johnny Chuck was fat and roly-poly. Reddy Fox was slim and wore a bright red coat. Reddy Fox used to like to frighten Johnny Chuck by suddenly popping out from behind a tree and making believe that he was going to eat Johnny Chuck all up.

One bright summer day Johnny Chuck was out looking for a good breakfast of nice tender clover. He had wandered quite a long way from his snug little house in the long meadow grass, although his mother had told him never to go out of sight of the door. But Johnny was like some little boys I know, and forgot all he had been told.

He walked and walked and walked. Every few minutes Johnny Chuck saw something farther on that looked like a patch of nice fresh clover. And every time when he reached it Johnny Chuck found that he had made a mistake. So Johnny Chuck walked and walked and walked.

Old Mother West Wind, coming across the Green Meadows, saw Johnny Chuck and asked him where he was going. Johnny Chuck pretended not to hear and just walked faster.

One of the Merry Little Breezes danced along in front of him.

"Look out, Johnny Chuck; you will get lost," cried the Merry Little Breeze, then pulled Johnny's whiskers and ran away.

Higher and higher up in the sky climbed round, red Mr. Sun. Every time Johnny Chuck looked up at him Mr. Sun winked.

"So long as I can see great round, red Mr. Sun and he winks at me I can't be lost," thought

Johnny Chuck, and trotted on looking for clover.

By and by Johnny Chuck really did find some clover—just the sweetest clover that grew in the Green Meadows. Johnny Chuck ate and ate and ate and then what do you think he did? Why, he curled right up in the nice sweet clover and went fast asleep.

Great round, red Mr. Sun kept climbing higher and higher up in the sky, then by and by he began to go down on the other side, and long shadows began to creep out across the Green Meadows. Johnny Chuck didn't know anything about them; he was fast asleep.

By and by one of the Merry Little Breezes found Johnny Chuck all curled up in a funny round ball.

"Wake up, Johnny Chuck! Wake up!" shouted the Merry Little Breeze.

Johnny Chuck opened his eyes. Then he sat up and rubbed them. For just a few, few minutes he couldn't remember where he was at all.

By and by he sat up very straight to look over the grass and see where he was. But he was so far from home that he didn't see a single thing that looked at all like the things he was used to. The trees were all different. The bushes were all different. Everything was different. Johnny Chuck was lost.

Now, when Johnny sat up, Reddy Fox happened to be looking over the Green Meadows and he saw Johnny's head where it popped above the grass.

"Aha!" said Reddy Fox, "I'll scare Johnny Chuck so he'll wish he'd never put his nose out of his house."

Then Reddy dropped down behind the long grass and crept softly, oh, ever so softly, through the paths of his own, until he was right behind Johnny Chuck. Johnny Chuck had been so intent looking for home that he didn't see anything else.

Reddy Fox stole right up behind Johnny and pulled Johnny's little short tail hard. How it did frighten Johnny Chuck! He jumped right straight

Johnny Chuck was lost. *Page 20.*

up in the air and when he came down he was the maddest little woodchuck that ever lived in the Green Meadows.

Reddy Fox had thought that Johnny would run, and then Reddy meant to run after him and pull his tail and tease him all the way home. Now, Reddy Fox got as big a surprise as Johnny had had when Reddy pulled his tail. Johnny didn't stop to think that Reddy Fox was twice as big as he, but, with his eyes snapping, and chattering as only a little Chuck can chatter, with every little hair on his little body standing right up on end, so that he seemed twice as big as he really was, he started for Reddy Fox.

It surprised Reddy Fox so that he didn't know what to do, and he simply ran. Johnny Chuck ran after him, nipping Reddy's heels every minute or two. Peter Rabbit just happened to be down that way. He was sitting up very straight looking to see what mischief he could get into when he caught sight of Reddy Fox running as hard as ever he could. "It must be that Bowser, the hound, is after

Reddy Fox," said Peter Rabbit to himself. "I must watch out that he doesn't find me."

Just then he caught sight of Johnny Chuck with every little hair standing up on end and running after Reddy Fox as fast as his short legs could go.

"Ho! ho! ho!" shouted Peter Rabbit. "Reddy Fox afraid of Johnny Chuck! Ho! ho! ho!"

Then Peter Rabbit scampered away to find Jimmy Skunk and Bobby Coon and Happy Jack Squirrel to tell them all about how Reddy Fox had run away from Johnny Chuck, for you see they were all a little afraid of Reddy Fox.

Straight home ran Reddy Fox as fast as he could go, and going home he passed the house of Johnny Chuck. Now Johnny couldn't run so fast as Reddy Fox and he was puffing and blowing as only a fat little woodchuck can puff and blow when he has to run hard. Moreover, he had lost his ill temper now and he thought it was the best joke ever to think that he had actually frightened Reddy Fox. When he came to his own house he stopped and sat on his hind legs once more. Then he shrilled out after Reddy Fox: "Reddy Fox is a 'fraid-cat, 'fraid-cat! Reddy Fox is a 'fraid-cat!"

And all the Merry Little Breezes of Old Mother West Wind, who were playing on the Green Meadows, shouted: "Reddy Fox is a 'fraid-cat, 'fraid-cat!"

And this is the way that Reddy Fox was surprised and that Johnny Chuck found his way home.

~

CHAPTER IV

WHY JIMMY SKUNK WEARS STRIPES

Jimmy Skunk, as everybody knows, wears a striped suit, a suit of black and white. There was a time, long, long ago, when all the Skunk family wore black. Very handsome their coats were, too, a beautiful, glossy black. They were very, very proud of them and took the greatest care of them, brushing them carefully ever so many times a day.

There was a Jimmy Skunk then, just as there is now, and he was head of all the Skunk family. Now this Jimmy Skunk was very proud and thought himself very much of a gentleman. He was very independent and cared for no one. Like a great many other independent people, he did not always consider the rights of others. Indeed, it was hinted in the wood and on the Green Meadows that not all of Jimmy Skunk's doings would bear the light of day. It was openly said that he was altogether too fond of prowling about at night, but no one could prove that he was responsible for mischief done in the night, for no one saw him. You see his coat was so black that in the darkness of the night it was not visible at all.

Now about this time of which I am telling you Mrs. Ruffed Grouse made a nest at the foot of the Great Pine and in it she laid fifteen beautiful buff eggs. Mrs. Grouse was very happy, very happy indeed, and all the little meadow folks who knew of her happiness were happy too, for they all loved shy, demure, little Mrs. Grouse. Every morning when Peter Rabbit trotted down the Lone Little Path through the wood past the Great Pine he would stop for a few minutes to chat with Mrs. Grouse. Happy Jack Squirrel would bring her the news every afternoon. The Merry Little Breezes of Old Mother West Wind would run up a dozen times a day to see how she was getting along.

One morning Peter Rabbit, coming down the Lone Little Path for his usual morning call, found a terrible state of affairs. Poor little Mrs. Grouse was heart-broken. All about the foot of the Great Pine lay the empty shells of her beautiful eggs. They had been broken and scattered this way and that.

"How did it happen?" asked Peter Rabbit.

"I don't know," sobbed poor little Mrs. Grouse. "In the night when I was fast asleep something pounced upon me. I managed to get away and fly up in the top of the Great Pine. In the morning I found all my eggs broken, just as you see them here."

Peter Rabbit looked the ground over very carefully. He hunted around behind the Great Pine, he looked under the bushes, he studied the ground with a very wise air. Then he hopped off down the Lone Little Path to the Green Meadows. He stopped at the house of Johnny Chuck.

"What makes your eyes so big and round?" asked Johnny Chuck.

Peter Rabbit came very close so as to whisper in Johnny Chuck's ear, and told him all that he had seen. Together they went to Jimmy Skunk's house. Jimmy Skunk was in bed. He was very sleepy and very cross when he came to the door. Peter Rabbit told him what he had seen.

"Too bad! Too bad!" said Jimmy Skunk, and yawned sleepily.

"Won't you join us in trying to find out who did it?" asked Johnny Chuck.

Jimmy Skunk said he would be delighted to come but that he had some other business that morning and that he would join them in the afternoon. Peter Rabbit and Johnny Chuck went on. Pretty soon they met the Merry Little Breezes and told them the dreadful story.

"What shall we do?" asked Johnny Chuck.

"We'll hurry over and tell Old Dame Nature," cried the Merry Little Breezes, "and ask her what to do."

So away flew the Merry Little Breezes to Old Dame Nature and told her all the dreadful story. Old Dame Nature listened very attentively. Then she sent the Merry Little Breezes to all the little meadow folks to tell every one to be at the Great Pine that afternoon. Now whatever Old Dame Nature commanded all the meadow folks were obliged to do. They did not dare to disobey her. Promptly at four o'clock that afternoon all the meadow folks were gathered around the foot of the Great Pine. Broken-hearted little Mrs. Ruffed Grouse sat beside her empty nest, with all the broken shells about her.

Reddy Fox, Peter Rabbit, Johnny Chuck, Billy Mink, Little Joe Otter, Jerry Muskrat, Hooty the Owl, Bobby Coon, Sammy Jay, Blacky the Crow, Grandfather Frog, Mr. Toad, Spotty the Turtle, the Merry Little Breezes, all were there. Last of all came Jimmy Skunk. Very handsome he looked in his shining black coat and very sorry he appeared that such a dreadful thing should have happened. He told Mrs. Grouse how badly he felt, and he loudly demanded that the culprit should be found out and severely punished.

Old Dame Nature has the most smiling face in the world, but this time it was very, very grave indeed. First she asked little Mrs. Grouse to tell her story all over again that all might hear. Then each in turn was asked to tell where he had been the night before. Johnny Chuck, Happy Jack Squirrel, Striped Chipmunk, Sammy Jay and Blacky the Crow had gone to bed when Mr. Sun went down behind the Purple Hills. Jerry Muskrat, Billy Mink, Little Joe Otter, Grandfather Frog and Spotty the Turtle, had not left the Smiling Pool. Bobby Coon had been down in Farmer Brown's cornfield. Hooty the Owl had been hunting in the lower end of the Green Meadows. Peter Rabbit had been down in the berry patch. Mr. Toad had been under the piece of bark which he called a house. Old Dame Nature called on Jimmy Skunk last of all. Jimmy protested that he had been very, very tired and had gone to bed very early indeed and had slept the whole night through.

Then Old Dame Nature asked Peter Rabbit what he had found among the egg shells that morning.

Peter Rabbit hopped out and laid three long black hairs before Old Dame Nature. "These," said Peter Rabbit "are what I found among the egg shells."

Then Old Dame Nature called Johnny Chuck. "Tell us, Johnny Chuck," said she, "what you saw when you called at Jimmy Skunk's house this morning."

"I saw Jimmy Skunk," said Johnny Chuck, "and Jimmy seemed very, very sleepy. It seemed to me that his whiskers were yellow."

"That will do," said Old Dame Nature, and then she called Old Mother West Wind.

"What time did you come down on the Green Meadows this morning?" asked Old Dame Nature.

"Just at the break of day," said Old Mother West Wind, "as Mr. Sun was coming up from behind the Purple Hills."

"And whom did you see so early in the morning?" asked Old Dame Nature.

"I saw Bobby Coon going home from old Farmer Brown's cornfield," said Old Mother West Wind. "I saw Hooty the Owl coming back from the lower end of the Green Meadows. I saw Peter Rabbit down in the berry patch. Last of all I saw something like a black shadow coming down the Lone Little Path toward the house of Jimmy Skunk."

Every one was looking very hard at Jimmy Skunk. Jimmy began to look very unhappy and very uneasy.

"Who wears a black coat?" asked Dame Nature.

"Jimmy Skunk!" shouted all the little meadow folks.

"What *might* make whiskers yellow?" asked Old Dame Nature.

No one seemed to know at first. Then Peter Rabbit spoke up. "It *might* be the yolk of an egg," said Peter Rabbit.

"Who are likely to be sleepy on a bright sunny morning?" asked Old Dame Nature.

"People who have been out all night," said Johnny Chuck, who himself always goes to bed with the sun.

"Jimmy Skunk," said Old Dame Nature, and her voice was very stern, very stern indeed, and her face was very grave. "Jimmy Skunk, I accuse you of having broken and eaten the eggs of Mrs. Grouse. What have you to say for yourself?"

Jimmy Skunk hung his head. He hadn't a word to say. He just wanted to sneak away by himself.

"Jimmy Skunk," said Old Dame Nature, "because your handsome black coat of which you are so proud has made it possible for you to move about in the night without being seen, and because we can no longer trust you upon your honor, henceforth you and your descendants shall wear a striped coat, which is the sign that you cannot be trusted. Your coat hereafter shall be black and white, that when you move about in the night you will always be visible."

And this is why that to this day Jimmy Skunk wears a striped suit of black and white.

CHAPTER V

∼

THE WILFUL LITTLE BREEZE

Old Mother West Wind was tired—tired and just a wee bit cross—cross because she was tired. She had had a very busy day. Ever since early morning she had been puffing out the white sales of the ships on the big ocean so that they might go faster; she had kept all the big and little wind mills whirling and whirling to pump water for thirsty folks and grind corn for hungry folks; she had blown away all the smoke from tall chimneys and engines and steamboats. Yes, indeed, Old Mother West Wind had been very, very busy.

Now she was coming across the Green Meadows on her way to her home behind the Purple

Hills, and as she came she opened the big bag she carried and called to her children, the Merry Little Breezes, who had been playing hard on the Green Meadows all the long day. One by one they crept into the big bag, for they were tired, too, and ready to go to their home behind the Purple Hills.

Pretty soon all were in the bag but one, a wilful little Breeze, who was not quite ready to go home; he wanted to play just a little longer. He danced ahead of Old Mother West Wind. He kissed the sleepy daisies. He shook the nodding buttercups. He set all the little poplar leaves a dancing, too, and he wouldn't come into the big bag. So Old Mother West Wind closed the big bag and slung it over her shoulder. Then she started on towards her home behind the Purple Hills.

When she had gone, the willful little Breeze left behind suddenly felt very lonely—very lonely indeed! The sleepy daisies didn't want to play. The nodding buttercups were cross. Great round bright Mr. Sun, who had been shining and shining all day long, went to bed and put on his night cap of golden clouds. Black shadows came creeping, creeping out into the Green Meadows.

The willful little Breeze began to wish that he was safe in Old Mother West Wind's big bag with all the other Merry Little Breezes.

So he started across the Green Meadows to find the Purple Hills. But all the hills were black now and he could not tell which he should look behind to find his home with Old Mother West Wind and the Merry Little Breezes. How he did wish that he had minded Old Mother West Wind.

By and by he curled up under a bayberry bush and tried to go to sleep, but he was lonely, oh, so lonely! And he couldn't go to sleep. Old Mother Moon came up and flooded all the Green Meadows with light, but it wasn't like the bright light of jolly round Mr. Sun, for it was cold and white and it made many black shadows.

Pretty soon the willful little Breeze heard Hooty the Owl out hunting for a meadow mouse for his dinner. Then down the Lone Little Path which ran close to the bayberry bush trotted Reddy Fox. He was trotting very softly and every minute or so he turned his head and looked behind him to see if he was followed. It was plain to see that Reddy Fox was bent on mischief.

When he reached the bayberry bush Reddy Fox sat down and barked twice. Hooty the Owl answered him at once and flew over to join him. They didn't see the willful little Breeze curled up under the bayberry bush, so intent were these two rogues in plotting mischief. They were planning to steal down across the Green Meadows to the edge of the Brown Pasture where Mr. Bob White and pretty Mrs. Bob White and a dozen little Bob Whites had their home.

"When they run along the ground I'll catch 'em, and when they fly up in the air you'll catch 'em, and we'll gobble 'em all up," said Reddy Fox to Hooty the Owl. Then he licked his chops and Hooty the Owl snapped his bill, just as if they were tasting tender little Bob Whites that very minute. It made the willful little Breeze shiver to see them. Pretty soon they started on towards the Brown Pasture.

When they were out of sight the willful little Breeze jumped up and shook himself. Then away he sped across the Green Meadows to the Brown Pasture. And because he could go faster and because he went a shorter way he got there first. He had to hunt and hunt to find Mrs. and Mr. Bob White and all the little Bob Whites, but finally he did find them, all with their heads tucked under their wings fast asleep.

The willful little Breeze shook Mr. Bob White very gently. In an instant he was wide awake.

"Sh-h-h," said the willful little Breeze. "Reddy Fox and Hooty the Owl are coming to the Brown Pasture to gobble up you and Mrs. Bob White and all the little Bob Whites."

"Thank you, little Breeze," said Mr. Bob White, "I think I'll move my family."

Then he woke Mrs. Bob White and all the little Bob Whites. With Mr. Bob White in the lead away they all flew to the far side of the Brown Pasture where they were soon safely hidden under a juniper tree.

The willful little Breeze saw them safely there, and when they were nicely hidden hurried back to the place where the Bob Whites had been sleeping. Reddy Fox was stealing up through the grass very, very softly. Hooty the Owl was flying as silently as a shadow. When Reddy Fox thought he was near enough he drew himself together, made a quick spring and landed right in Mr. Bob White's empty bed. Reddy Fox and Hooty the Owl looked so surprised and foolish when they found that the Bob Whites were not there that the willful little Breeze nearly laughed out loud.

Then Reddy Fox and Hooty the Owl hunted here and hunted there, all over the Brown Pasture, but they couldn't find the Bob Whites.

And the willful little Breeze went back to the juniper tree and curled himself beside Mr. Bob White to sleep, for he was lonely no longer.

CHAPTER VI

~

REDDY FOX GOES FISHING

One morning when Mr. Sun was very, very bright and it was very, very warm, down on the Green Meadows Reddy Fox came hopping and skipping down the Lone Little Path that leads to the Laughing Brook. Hoppity, skip, skippity hop! Reddy felt very much pleased with himself that sunny morning. Pretty soon he saw Johnny Chuck sitting up very straight close by the little house where he lives.

"Johnny Chuck, Chuck, Chuck! Johnny Chuck, Chuck, Chuck! Johnny Woodchuck!" called Reddy fox.

Johnny Chuck pretended not to hear. His mother had told him not to play with Reddy Fox, for Reddy Fox was a bad boy.

"Johnny Chuck, Chuck, Chuck! Johnny Wood-chuck!" called Reddy again.

This time Johnny turned and looked. He could see Reddy Fox turning somersaults and chasing his tail and rolling over and over in the little path.

"Come on!" said Reddy Fox. "Let's go fishing!"

"Can't," said Johnny Chuck, because, you know, his mother had told him not to play with Reddy Fox.

"I'll show you how to catch a fish," said Reddy Fox, and tried to jump over his own shadow.

"Can't," said good little Johnny Chuck again, and turned away so that he couldn't see Reddy Fox chasing Butterflies and playing catch with Field Mice children.

So Reddy Fox went down to the Laughing Brook all alone. The Brook was laughing and singing on its way to join the Big River. The sky was blue and the sun was bright. Reddy Fox jumped on the Big Rock in the middle of the Laughing Brook and peeped over the other side. What do you think he saw? Why, right down below in a

Dear Little Pool were Mr. and Mrs. Trout and all the little Trouts.

Reddy Fox wanted some of those little Trouts to take home for his dinner, but he didn't know how to catch them. He lay flat down on the Big Rock and reached way down into the Dear Little Pool, but all the little Trouts laughed at Reddy Fox and not one came within reach. Then Mr. Trout swam up so quickly that Reddy Fox didn't see him coming and bit Reddy's little black paw hard.

"Ouch!" cried Reddy Fox, pulling his little black paw out of the water. And all the little Trouts laughed at Reddy Fox.

Just then along came Billy Mink.

"Hello, Reddy Fox!" said Billy Mink. "What are you doing here?"

"I'm trying to catch a fish," said Reddy Fox.

"Pooh! That's easy!" said Billy Mink. "I'll show you how."

So Billy Mink lay down on the Big Rock side of Reddy Fox and peeped over into the Dear Little Pool where all the little Trouts were laughing at

43

Reddy Fox and having such a good time. But Billy Mink took care, such very great care, that Mr. Trout and Mrs. Trout should not see him peeping over into the Dear Little Pool.

When Billy Mink saw all those little Trouts playing in the Dear Little Pool he laughed. "You count three, Reddy Fox," said he, "and I'll show you how to catch a fish."

"One!" said Reddy Fox, "Two! Three!"

Splash! Billy Mink had dived head first into the Dear Little Pool. He spattered water way up onto Reddy Fox, and he frightened old Mr. Frog so that he fell over backwards off the lily pad where he was taking a morning nap right into the water. In a minute Billy Mink climbed out on the other side of the Dear Little Pool and sure enough, he had caught one of the little Trouts.

"Give it to me," cried Reddy Fox.

"Catch one yourself," said Billy Mink. "Old Grandpa Mink wants a fish for his dinner, so I am going to take this home. You're afraid, Reddy Fox! Fraid-cat! Fraid-cat!"

Billy Mink shook the water off of his little brown coat, picked up the little Trout and ran off home.

Reddy Fox lay down again on the Big Rock and peeped into the Dear Little Pool. Not a single Trout could he see. They were all hiding safely with Mr. and Mrs. Trout. Reddy Fox watched and watched. The sun was warm, the Laughing Brook was singing a lullaby and—what do you think? Why, Reddy Fox went fast asleep on the edge of the great Big Rock.

By and by Reddy Fox began to dream. He dreamed that he had a nice little brown coat that was waterproof, just like the little brown coat that Billy Mink wore. Yes, and he dreamed that he had learned to swim and to catch fish just as Billy Mink did. He dreamed that the Dear Little Pool was full of little Trouts and that he was just going to catch one when—splash! Reddy Fox had rolled right off of the Big Rock into the Dear Little Pool.

The water went into the eyes of Reddy Fox, and it went up his nose and he swallowed so much that he felt as if he never, never would want another drink of water. And his beautiful red coat, which old Mother Fox had told him to be very, very careful of because he couldn't have another for a whole year, was oh so wet! And his pants were wet and his beautiful bushy tail, of which he was so proud, was so full of water that he couldn't hold it up, but had to drag it up the bank after him as he crawled out of the Dear Little Pool.

"Ha! Ha! Ha!" laughed Mr. Kingfisher, sitting on a tree.

"Ho! Ho! Ho!" laughed old Mr. Frog, who had climbed back on his lily pad.

"He! He! He!" laughed all the little Trouts and Mr. Trout and Mrs. Trout, swimming round and round in the Dear Little Pool.

"Ha! Ha! Ha! Ho! Ho! Ho! He! He! He!" laughed Billy Mink, who had come back to the Big Rock just in time to see Reddy Fox tumble in.

Reddy Fox didn't say a word, he was so ashamed. He just crept up the Lone Little Path to his home, dragging his tail, all wet and muddy, behind him, and dripping water all the way.

Johnny Chuck was still sitting by his door as his mother had told him to. Reddy Fox tried to go past without being seen, but Johnny Chuck's bright little eyes saw him.

"Where are your fish, Reddy Fox?" called Johnny Chuck.

Reddy Fox said never a word, but walked faster.

"Why don't you turn somersaults, and jump over your shadow and chase Butterflies and play with the little Field Mice, Reddy Fox?" called Johnny Chuck.

But Reddy Fox just walked faster. When he got almost home he saw old Mother Fox sitting in the doorway with a great big switch across her lap, for Mother Fox had told Reddy Fox not to go near the Laughing Brook.

And this is all I am going to tell you about how Reddy Fox went fishing.

CHAPTER VII

~

JIMMY SKUNK LOOKS FOR BEETLES

Jimmy Skunk opened his eyes very early one morning and peeped out of his snug little house on the hill. Big, round Mr. Sun, with a very red, smiling face, had just begun to climb up into the sky. Old Mother West Wind was just starting down to the Green Meadows with her big bag over her shoulder. In that bag Jimmy Skunk knew she carried all her children, the Merry Little Breezes, whom she was taking down to the Green Meadows to play and frolic all day.

"Good morning, Mother West Wind," said Jimmy Skunk, politely. "Did you see any beetles as you came down the hill?"

Old Mother West Wind said, no, she hadn't seen any beetles as she came down the hill.

"Thank you," said Jimmy Skunk politely. "I guess I'll have to go look myself, for I'm very, very hungry."

So Jimmy Skunk brushed his handsome black and white coat, and washed his face and hands, and started out to try to find some beetles for his breakfast. First he went down to the Green Meadows and stopped at Johnny Chuck's house. But Johnny Chuck was still in bed and fast asleep. Then Jimmy Skunk went over to see if Reddy Fox would go with him to help find some beetles for his breakfast. But Reddy Fox had been out very, very late the night before and was still in bed fast asleep, too.

So Jimmy Skunk set out all alone along the Crooked Little Path up the hill to find some beetles for his breakfast. He walked very slowly, for Jimmy Skunk never hurries. He stopped and peeped under every old log to see if there were any beetles. By and by he came to a big piece of bark beside the Crooked Little Path. Jimmy Skunk took hold of the piece of bark with his two little black paws and pulled and pulled. All of a sudden, the big piece of bark turned over so quickly that Jimmy Skunk fell flat on his back.

When Jimmy Skunk had rolled over onto his feet again, there sat old Mr. Toad right in the path, and old Mr. Toad was very, very cross indeed. He swelled and he puffed and he puffed and he swelled, till he was twice as big as Jimmy Skunk had ever seen him before.

"Good morning, Mr. Toad," said Jimmy Skunk. "Have you seen any beetles?"

But Mr. Toad blinked his great round goggly eyes and he said:

"What do you mean, Jimmy Skunk, by pulling the roof off my house?"

"Is that the roof of your house?" asked Jimmy Skunk politely. "I won't do it again."

Then Jimmy Skunk stepped right over old Mr. Toad, and went on up the Crooked Little Path to look for some beetles.

By and by he came to an old stump of a tree which was hollow and had the nicest little round hole in one side. Jimmy Skunk took hold of one edge with his two little black paws and pulled and pulled. All of a sudden the whole side of the old stump tore open and Jimmy Skunk fell flat on his back.

When Jimmy Skunk had rolled over onto his feet again there was Striped Chipmunk hopping up and down right in the middle of the path, he was so angry.

"Good morning, Striped Chipmunk," said Jimmy Skunk. "Have you seen any beetles?"

But Striped Chipmunk hopped faster than ever and he said:

"What do you mean, Jimmy Skunk, by pulling the side off my house?"

"Is that the side of your house?" asked Jimmy Skunk, politely. "I won't do it again."

Then Jimmy Skunk stepped right over Striped Chipmunk, and went on up the Crooked Little Path to look for some beetles.

Pretty soon he met Peter Rabbit hopping along down the Crooked Little Path. "Good morning,

Jimmy Skunk, where are you going so early in the morning?" said Peter Rabbit.

"Good morning, Peter Rabbit. Have you seen any beetles?" asked Jimmy Skunk, politely.

"No, I haven't seen any beetles, but I'll help you find some," said Peter Rabbit. So he turned about and hopped ahead of Jimmy Skunk up the Crooked Little Path.

Now because Peter Rabbit's legs are long and he is always in a hurry, he got to the top of the hill first. When Jimmy Skunk reached the end of the Crooked Little Path on the top of the hill he found Peter Rabbit sitting up very straight and looking and looking very hard at a great flat stone.

"What are you looking at, Peter Rabbit?" asked Jimmy Skunk.

"Sh-h-h!" said Peter Rabbit, "I think there are some beetles under that great flat stone where that little black string is sticking out. Now when I count three you grab that string and pull hard; perhaps you'll find a beetle at the other end."

So Jimmy Skunk got ready and Peter Rabbit began to count.

"One!" said Peter. "Two!" said Peter. "Three!"

Jimmy Skunk grabbed the black string and pulled as hard as ever he could and out came— Mr. Black Snake! The string Jimmy Skunk had pulled was Mr. Black Snake's tail, and Mr. Black Snake was very, very angry indeed.

"Ha! Ha! Ha!" laughed Peter Rabbit.

"What do you mean, Jimmy Skunk," said Mr. Black Snake, "by pulling my tail?"

"Was that your tail?" said Jimmy Skunk, politely. "I won't do it again. Have you seen any beetles?"

But Mr. Black Snake hadn't seen any beetles, and he was so cross that Jimmy Skunk went on over the hill to look for some beetles.

Peter Rabbit was still laughing and laughing and laughing. And the more he laughed the angrier grew Mr. Black Snake, till finally he started after Peter Rabbit to teach him a lesson.

Then Peter Rabbit stopped laughing, for Mr. Black Snake can run very fast. Away went Peter

Rabbit down the Crooked Little Path as fast as he could go, and away went Mr. Black Snake after him.

But Jimmy Skunk didn't even look once to see if Mr. Black Snake had caught Peter Rabbit to teach him a lesson, for Jimmy Skunk had found some beetles and was eating his breakfast.

CHAPTER VIII

~

BILLY MINK'S SWIMMING PARTY

B illy Mink was coming down the bank of the Laughing Brook. Billy Mink was feeling very good indeed. He had had a good breakfast, the sun was warm, little white cloud ships were sailing across the blue sky and their shadows were sailing across the Green Meadows, the birds were singing and the bees were humming. Billy Mink felt like singing too, but Billy Mink's voice was not meant for singing.

By and by Billy Mink came to the Smiling Pool. Here the Laughing Brook stopped and rested on its way to join the Big River. It stopped its noisy laughing and singing and just lay smiling and smiling in the warm sunshine. The little flowers on the bank leaned over and nodded to it. The beech tree, which was very old, sometimes dropped a leaf into it. The cat-tails kept their feet cool in the edge of it.

Billy Mink jumped out on the Big Rock and looked down into the Smiling Pool. Over on a green lily pad he saw old Grandfather Frog.

"Hello, Grandfather Frog," said Billy Mink.

"Hello, Billy Mink," said Grandfather Frog. "What mischief are you up to this fine sunny morning?"

Just then Billy Mink saw a little brown head swimming along one edge of the Smiling Pool.

"Hello, Jerry Muskrat!" shouted Billy Mink.

"Hello your own self, Billy Mink," shouted Jerry Muskrat, "Come in and have a swim; the water's fine!"

"Good," said Billy Mink. "We'll have a swimming party."

So Billy Mink called all the Merry Little Breezes of Old Mother West Wind, who were playing with the flowers on the bank, and sent them to find Little Joe Otter and invite him to come to the swimming party. Pretty soon back came the Little Breezes and with them came Little Joe Otter.

"Hello, Billy Mink," said Little Joe Otter. "Here I am!"

"Hello, Little Joe Otter," said Billy Mink. "Come up here on the Big Rock and see who can dive the deepest into the Smiling Pool."

So Little Joe Otter and Jerry Muskrat climbed up on the Big Rock side of Billy Mink and they all stood side by side in their little brown bathing suits looking down into the Smiling Pool.

"Now when I count three we'll all dive into the Smiling Pool together and see who can dive the deepest. One!" said Billy Mink. "Two!" said Billy Mink. "Three!" said Billy Mink.

And when he said "Three!" in they all went head first. My such a splash as they did make! They upset old Grandfather Frog so that he fell off his lily pad. They frightened Mr. and Mrs. Trout so that they jumped right out of the water. Tiny Tadpole had such a scare that he hid way, way down in the mud with only the tip of his funny little nose sticking out.

"Chug-a-rum," said old Grandfather Frog, climbing out of his lily pad. "If I wasn't so old I would show you how to dive."

"Come on, Grandfather Frog!" cried Billy Mink. "Show us how to dive."

And what do you think? Why, old Grandfather Frog actually got so excited that he climbed up on the Big Rock to show them how to dive. Splash! Went Grandfather Frog into the Smiling Pool. Splash! Went Billy Mink right behind him. Splash! Splash! Went Little Joe Otter and Jerry Muskrat, right at Billy Mink's heels.

"Hurrah!" shouted Mr. Kingfisher, sitting on a branch of the old beech tree. And then just to show them that he could dive, too, splash! he went into the Smiling Pool.

Such a noise as they did make! All the Little Breezes of Old Mother West Wind danced for joy on the bank. Blacky the Crow and Sammy Jay flew over to see what was going on.

"Now let's see who can swim the farthest under water," cried Billy Mink.

So they all stood side by side on one edge of the Smiling Pool.

"Go!" shouted Mr. Kingfisher, and in they all plunged. Little ripples ran across the Smiling Pool and then the water became as smooth and smiling as if nothing had gone into it with a plunge.

Now old Grandfather Frog began to realize that he wasn't as young as he used to be, and he couldn't swim as fast as the others anyway. He began to get short of breath, so he swam up to the top and stuck just the tip of his nose out to get some more air. Sammy Jay's sharp eyes saw him.

"There's Grandfather Frog!" he shouted.

So then Grandfather Frog popped his head out and swam over to his green lily pad to rest.

Way over beyond the Big Rock little bubbles in three long rows kept coming up to the top of the Smiling Pool. They showed just where Billy Mink, Little Joe Otter and Jerry Muskrat were swimming way down out of sight. It was the air from their lungs making the bubbles. Straight across the Smiling Pool went the lines of little bubbles and then way out on the farther side two little heads bobbed out of water close together. They were Billy Mink and Little Joe Otter. A moment later Jerry Muskrat bobbed up beside them.

You see, they had swum clear across the Smiling Pool and of course they could swim no farther.

So Billy Mink's swimming party was a great success.

CHAPTER IX

~

PETER RABBIT PLAYS A JOKE

One morning when big round Mr. Sun was climbing up in the sky and Old Mother West Wind had sent all her Merry Little Breezes to play in the Green Meadows, Johnny Chuck started out for a walk. First he sat up very straight and looked and looked all around to see if Reddy Fox was anywhere about, for you know Reddy Fox liked to tease Johnny Chuck.

But Reddy Fox was nowhere to be seen, so Johnny Chuck trotted down the Lone Little Path to the wood. Mr. Sun was shining as brightly as ever he could and Johnny Chuck, who was very, very fat, grew very, very warm. By and by he sat down on the end of a log under a big tree to rest.

Thump! Something hit Johnny Chuck right on the top of his round little head. It made Johnny Chuck jump.

"Hello, Johnny Chuck!" said a voice that seemed to come right out of the sky. Johnny Chuck tipped his head way, way back and looked up. He was just in time to see Happy Jack Squirrel drop a nut. Down it came and hit Johnny Chuck right on the tip of his funny, black, little nose.

"Oh!" said Johnny Chuck, and tumbled right over back off the log. But Johnny Chuck was so round and so fat and so roly-poly that it didn't hurt him a bit.

"Ha! Ha! Ha!" laughed Happy Jack up in the tree.

"Ha! Ha! Ha!" laughed Johnny Chuck, picking himself up. Then they both laughed together. It was such a good joke.

"What are you laughing at?" asked a voice so close to Johnny Chuck that he rolled over three times he was so surprised. It was Peter Rabbit.

"What are you doing in my wood?" asked Peter Rabbit.

"I'm taking a walk," said Johnny Chuck.

"Good," said Peter Rabbit, "I'll come along too."

So Johnny Chuck and Peter Rabbit set out along the Lone Little Path through the wood. Peter Rabbit hopped along with great big jumps, for Peter's legs are long and meant for jumping, but Johnny Chuck couldn't keep up though he tried very hard, for Johnny's legs are short. Pretty soon Peter Rabbit came back, walking very softly. He whispered in Johnny Chuck's ear.

"I've found something," said Peter Rabbit.

"What is it?" asked Johnny Chuck.

"I'll show you," said Peter Rabbit, "but you must be very, very still, and not make the least little bit of noise."

Johnny Chuck promised to be very, very still for he wanted very much to see what Peter Rabbit had found. Peter Rabbit tip-toed down the Lone Little Path through the wood, his funny long ears pointing right up to the sky. And behind him tip-toed

Johnny Chuck, wondering and wondering what it could be that Peter Rabbit had found.

Pretty soon they came to a nice mossy green log right across the Lone Little Path. Peter Rabbit stopped and sat up very straight. He looked this way and looked that way. Johnny Chuck stopped too and he sat up very straight and looked this way and looked that way, but all he could see was the mossy green log across the Lone Little Path.

"What is it, Peter Rabbit?" whispered Johnny Chuck.

"You can't see it yet," whispered Peter Rabbit, "for first we have to jump over that mossy green log. Now I'll jump first, and then you jump just the way I do, and then you'll see what it is I've found," said Peter Rabbit.

So Peter Rabbit jumped first, and because his legs are long and meant for jumping, he jumped way, way over the mossy green log. Then he turned around and sat up to see Johnny Chuck jump over the mossy green log, too.

Johnny Chuck tried to jump very high and very far, just as he had seen Peter Rabbit jump, but Johnny Chuck's legs are very short and not meant for jumping. Besides, Johnny Chuck was very, very fat. So though he tried very hard indeed to jump just like Peter Rabbit, he stubbed his toes on the top of the mossy green log and over he tumbled, head first, and landed with a great big thump right on Reddy Fox, who was lying fast asleep on the other side of the mossy green log.

Peter Rabbit laughed and laughed until he had to hold his sides.

My, how frightened Johnny Chuck was when he saw what he had done! Before he could get on his feet he had rolled right over behind a little bush, and there he lay very, very still.

Reddy Fox awoke with a grunt when Johnny Chuck fell on him so hard, and the first thing he saw was Peter Rabbit laughing so that he had to hold his sides. Reddy Fox didn't stop to look around. He thought that Peter Rabbit had jumped on him. Up jumped Reddy Fox and away ran Peter Rabbit. Away went Reddy Fox after Peter Rabbit. Peter dodged behind the trees, and jumped over the bushes, and ran this way and ran that way, just as hard as ever he could, for Peter Rabbit was very much afraid of Reddy Fox. And Reddy Fox followed Peter Rabbit behind the trees and over the bushes this way and that way, but he couldn't catch Peter Rabbit. Pretty soon Peter Rabbit came to the house of Jimmy Skunk. He knew that Jimmy Skunk was over in the pasture, so he popped right in and then he was safe, for the door of Jimmy Skunk's house was too small for Reddy Fox to squeeze in. Reddy Fox sat down and waited, but Peter Rabbit didn't come out. By and by Reddy Fox gave it up and trotted off home where old Mother Fox was waiting for him.

All this time Johnny Chuck had sat very still, watching Reddy Fox try to catch Peter Rabbit. And when he saw Peter Rabbit pop into the house of Jimmy Skunk and Reddy Fox trot away home, Johnny Chuck stood up and brushed his little

The door of Jimmy Skunk's house was too
small for Reddy Fox to squeeze in. *Page 68.*

coat very clean and then he trotted back up the Lone Little Path through the wood to his own dear little path through the Green Meadows where the Merry Little Breezes of Old Mother West Wind were still playing, till he was safe in his own snug little house once more.

CHAPTER X

~

HOW SAMMY JAY WAS FOUND OUT

Sammy Jay was very busy, very busy indeed. When anyone happened that way Sammy Jay pretended to be doing nothing at all, for Sammy Jay thought himself a very fine gentleman. He was very proud of his handsome blue coat with white trimmings and his high cap, and he would sit on a fence post and make fun of Johnny Chuck working at a new door for his snug little home in the Green Meadows, and of Striped Chipmunk storing up heaps of corn and nuts for the winter, for most of the time Sammy Jay was an idle fellow. And when Sammy Jay *was* busy, he was pretty sure to be doing something that he ought not to do, for idle people almost always get into mischief.

Sammy Jay was in mischief now, and that is why he pretended to be doing nothing when he thought any one was looking.

Old Mother West Wind had come down from her home behind the Purple Hills very early that morning. Indeed, jolly, round, red Mr. Sun had hardly gotten out of bed when she crossed the Green Meadows on her way to help the big ships across the ocean. Old Mother West Wind's eyes were sharp, and she saw Sammy Jay before Sammy Jay saw her.

"Now what can Sammy Jay be so busy about, and why is he so very, very quiet?" thought Old Mother West Wind. "He must be up to some mischief."

So when she opened her big bag and turned out all her Merry Little Breezes to play on the Green Meadows she sent one of them to see what Sammy Jay was doing in the old chestnut tree. The Merry Little Breeze danced along over the tree tops just as if he hadn't a thought in the world but to wake up all the little leaves and set them to dancing too, and Sammy Jay, watching Old Mother West Wind and the other Merry Little Breezes, didn't see this Merry Little Breeze at all.

Pretty soon it danced back to Old Mother West Wind and whispered in her ear: "Sammy Jay is stealing the nuts Happy Jack Squirrel had hidden in the hollow of the old chestnut tree, and is hiding them for himself in the tumble down nest that Blacky the Crow built in the Great Pine last year." "Aha!" said Old Mother West Wind. Then she went on across the Green Meadows.

"Good morning, Old Mother West Wind," said Sammy Jay as she passed the fence post where he was sitting.

"Good morning, Sammy Jay," said Old Mother West Wind. "What brings you out so early in the morning?"

"I'm out for my health, Old Mother West Wind," said Sammy Jay politely. "The doctor has ordered me to take a bath in the dew at sunrise every morning."

Old Mother West Wind said nothing, but went on her way across the Green Meadows to blow the ships across the ocean. When she had passed, Sammy Jay hurried to take the last of Happy Jack's nuts to the old nest in the Great Pine.

Poor Happy Jack! Soon he came dancing along with another nut to put in the hollow of the old chestnut tree. When he peeped in and saw that all his big store of nuts had disappeared, he couldn't believe his own eyes. He put in one paw and felt all around but not a nut could he feel. Then he climbed in and sure enough, the hollow was empty.

Poor Happy Jack! There were tears in his eyes when he crept out again. He looked all around but no one was to be seen but handsome Sammy Jay, very busy brushing his beautiful blue coat.

"Good morning, Sammy Jay, have you seen anyone pass this way?" asked Happy Jack. "Someone has stolen a store of nuts from the hollow in the old chestnut tree."

Sammy Jay pretended to feel very badly indeed, and in his sweetest voice, for his voice was very sweet in those days, he offered to help Happy Jack try to catch the thief who had stolen the store of nuts from the hollow in the old chestnut tree.

Together they went down across the Green Meadows asking every one whom they met if they had seen the thief who had stolen Happy Jack's store of nuts from the hollow in the old chestnut tree. All the Merry Little Breezes joined in the search, and soon everyone who lived in the Green Meadows or in the wood knew that someone had stolen all of Happy Jack Squirrel's store of nuts from the hollow in the old chestnut tree. And because every one liked Happy Jack, everyone felt very sorry indeed for him.

The next morning all the Merry Little Breezes of Old Mother West Wind were turned out of the big bag into the Green Meadows very early in-deed, for they had a lot of errands to do. All over the Green Meadows they hurried, all through the wood, up and down the Laughing Brook and all around the Smiling Pool, inviting everybody to meet at the Great Pine on the hill at nine o'clock to form a committee of the whole—that's what Old Mother West Wind called it—a committee of the whole—to try to find the thief who stole Happy Jack's nuts from the hollow in the old chestnut tree.

And because every one liked Happy Jack everyone went to the Great Pine on the hill— Reddy Fox, Bobby Coon, Jimmy Skunk, Striped Chipmunk, who is Happy Jack's cousin you know, Billy Mink, Little Joe Otter, Jerry Muskrat, Hooty the Owl, who was almost too sleepy to keep his eyes open, Blacky the Crow, Johnny Chuck, Peter Rabbit, even old Grandfather Frog. Of course Sammy Jay was there, looking his handsomest.

When they had all gathered around the Great Pine, Old Mother West Wind pointed to the old nest way up in the top of it. "Is that your nest?" she asked Blacky the Crow.

"It was, but I gave it to my cousin, Sammy Jay," said Blacky the Crow.

"Is that your nest, and may I have a stick out of it?" asked Old Mother West Wind of Sammy Jay.

"It is," said Sammy Jay, with his politest bow, "And you are welcome to a stick out of it." To himself he thought, "She will only take one from the top and that won't matter."

Old Mother West Wind suddenly puffed out her cheeks and blew so hard that she blew a big stick right out of the bottom of the old nest. Down it fell bumpity-bump on the branches of the Great Pine. After it fell—what do you think? Why, hickory nuts and chestnuts and acorns and hazel nuts, such a lot of them!

"Why! Why—e—e!" cried Happy Jack. "There are all my stolen nuts!"

Everybody turned to look at Sammy Jay, but he was flying off through the wood as fast as he could go. "Stop thief!" cried Old Mother West Wind. "Stop thief!" cried all the Merry Little

Breezes and Johnny Chuck and Billy Mink and all the rest. But Sammy Jay didn't stop.

Then all began to pick up the nuts that had fallen from the old nest where Sammy Jay had hidden them. By and by, with Happy Jack leading the way, they all marched back to the old chestnut tree and there Happy Jack stored all the nuts away in his snug little hollow once more.

And ever since that day, Sammy Jay, whenever he tries to call, just screams" "Thief!" "Thief!" "Thief!"

CHAPTER XI

~

JERRY MUSKRAT'S PARTY

All the Merry Little Breezes of Old Mother West Wind were hurrying over the Green Meadows. Some flew this way and some ran that way and some danced the other way. You see, Jerry Muskrat had asked them to carry his invitations to a party at the Big Rock in the Smiling Pool.

Of course everyone said that they would be delighted to go to Jerry Muskrat's party. Round Mr. Sun shone his very brightest. The sky was its bluest and the little birds had promised to be there to sing for Jerry Muskrat, so of course all the little folks in the Green Meadows and in the wood wanted to go.

There were Johnny Chuck and Reddy Fox and Jimmy Skunk and Bobby Coon and Happy Jack Squirrel and Striped Chipmunk and Billy Mink and Little Joe Otter and Grandfather Frog and old Mr. Toad and Mr. Blacksnake—all going to Jerry Muskrat's party.

When they reached the Smiling Pool they found Jerry Muskrat all ready. His brothers and his sister, his aunts and his uncles and his cousins were all there. Such a merry, merry time as there was in the Smiling Pool! How the water did splash! Billy Mink and Little Joe Otter and Grandfather Frog jumped right in as soon as they got there. They played tag in the water and hid behind the Big Rock. They turned somersaults down the slippery slide and they had such a good time!

But Reddy Fox and Peter Rabbit and Bobby Coon and Johnny Chuck and Jimmy Skunk and Happy Jack and Striped Chipmunk couldn't swim, so of course they couldn't play tag in the water or hide and seek or go down the slippery slide; all they could do was sit around to look on and wish that they knew how to swim, too. So of course they didn't have a good time. Soon they began to wish that they hadn't come to Jerry Muskrat's party. When he found that they were not having a good time, poor Jerry Muskrat felt very badly indeed. You see he lives in the water so much that he had quite forgotten that there was anyone who couldn't swim, or he never, never would have invited all the little meadow folks who live on dry land.

"Let's go home," said Peter Rabbit to Johnny Chuck.

"We can have more fun up on the hill," said Jimmy Skunk.

Just then Little Joe Otter came pushing a great big log across the Smiling Pool.

"Here's a ship, Bobby Coon. You get on one end and I'll give you a sail across the Smiling Pool," shouted Little Joe Otter.

So Bobby Coon crawled out on the big log and held on very tight, while little Joe Otter swam behind and pushed the big log. Across the Smiling Pool they went and back again. Bobby

Coon had such a good ride that he wanted to go again, but Jimmy Skunk wanted a ride. So Bobby Coon hopped off of the big log and Jimmy Skunk hopped on and away he went across the Smiling Pool with little Joe Otter pushing behind.

Then Jerry Muskrat found another log and gave Peter Rabbit a ride. Jerry Muskrat's brothers and sisters and aunts and uncles and cousins found logs and took Reddy Fox and Johnny Chuck and even Mr. Toad back and forth across the Smiling Pool.

Happy Jack Squirrel sat up very straight on the end of his log and spread his great bushy tail for a sail. All the little Breezes blew and blew and Happy Jack Squirrel sailed round and round the Smiling Pool.

Sometimes someone would fall off into the water and get wet, but Jerry Muskrat or Billy Mink always pulled them out again, and no one cared the tiniest bit for a wetting.

In the bushes around the Smiling Pool the little birds sang and sang. Reddy Fox barked his loudest. Happy Jack Squirrel chattered and chir—r—r—ed. All the muskrats squealed and squeaked, for Jerry Muskrat's party was such fun!

By and by when Mr. Sun went down behind the Purple Hills to his home and Old Mother West Wind with all her Merry Little Breezes went after him, and the little stars came out to twinkle and twinkle, the Smiling Pool lay all quiet and still, but smiling and smiling to think what a good time every one had had at Jerry Muskrat's party.

CHAPTER XII

~

BOBBY COON AND REDDY FOX PLAY TRICKS

It was night. All the little stars were looking down and twinkling and twinkling. Mother Moon was doing her best to make the Green Meadows as light as Mr. Sun did in the daytime. All the little birds except Hooty the Owl and Boomer the Night Hawk, and noisy Mr. Whip-poor-will were fast asleep in their little nests. Old Mother West Wind's Merry Little Breezes had all gone to sleep, too. It was oh so still! Indeed it was so very still that Bobby Coon, coming down the Lone Little Path through the wood, began to talk to himself.

"I don't see what people want to play all day and sleep all night for," said Bobby Coon.

"Night's the best time to be about. Now Reddy Fox—"

"Be careful what you say about Reddy Fox," said a voice right behind Bobby Coon.

Bobby Coon turned around very quickly indeed, for he had thought he was all alone. There was Reddy Fox himself, trotting down the Lone Little Path through the wood.

"I thought you were home and fast asleep, Reddy Fox," said Bobby Coon.

"You were mistaken," said Reddy Fox. "For you see I'm out to take a walk in the moonlight."

So Bobby Coon and Reddy Fox walked together down the Lone Little Path through the wood to the Green Meadows. They met Jimmy Skunk, who had dreamed that there were a lot of beetles up on the hill, and was just going to climb the Crooked Little Path to see.

"Hello, Jimmy Skunk!" said Bobby Coon and Reddy Fox. "Come down to the Green Meadows with us."

Jimmy Skunk said he would, so they all went down on the Green Meadows together, Bobby

Coon first, Reddy Fox next and Jimmy Skunk last of all, for Jimmy Skunk never hurries. Pretty soon they came to the house of Johnny Chuck.

"Listen," said Bobby Coon. "Johnny Chuck is fast asleep."

They all listened and they could hear Johnny Chuck snoring away down in his snug little bed.

"Let's give Johnny Chuck a surprise," said Reddy Fox.

"What shall it be?" asked Bobby Coon.

"I know," said Reddy Fox. "Let's roll that big stone right over Johnny Chuck's doorway; then he'll have to dig his way out in the morning."

So Bobby Coon and Reddy Fox pulled and tugged and tugged and pulled at the big stone till they had rolled it over Johnny Chuck's doorway. Jimmy Skunk pretended not to see what they were doing.

"Now let's go down to the Laughing Brook and wake up old Grandfather Frog and hear him say 'Chug-a-rum,'" said Bobby Coon.

"Come on!" cried Reddy Fox, "I'll get there first!"

Away raced Reddy Fox down the Lone Little Path and after him ran Bobby Coon, going to wake old Grandfather Frog from a nice comfortable sleep on his green lily pad.

But Jimmy Skunk didn't go. He watched Reddy Fox and Bobby Coon until they were nearly to the Laughing Brook. Then he began to dig at one side of the big stone which filled the doorway of Johnny Chuck's house. My, how he made the dirt fly! Pretty soon he had made a hole big enough to call through to Johnny Chuck, who was snoring away, fast asleep in his snug little bed below.

"Johnny Chuck, Chuck, Chuck! Johnny Woodchuck!" called Jimmy Skunk.

But Johnny Chuck just snored.

"Johnny Chuck, Chuck, Chuck! Johnny Woodchuck!" called Jimmy Skunk once more.

But Johnny Chuck just snored. Then Jimmy Skunk called again, this time louder than before.

"Who is it?" asked a very sleepy voice.

"It's Jimmy Skunk. Put your coat on and come up here!" called Jimmy Skunk.

"Go away, Jimmy Skunk. I want to sleep!" said Johnny Chuck.

"I've got a surprise for you, Johnny Chuck. You'd better come!" called Jimmy Skunk through the little hole he had made. When Johnny Chuck heard that Jimmy Skunk had a surprise for him he wanted to know right away what it could be, so though he was very, very sleepy, he put on his coat and started up for his door to see what the surprise was that Jimmy Skunk had. And there he found the big stone Reddy Fox and Bobby Coon had put there, and of course he was very much surprised indeed. He thought Jimmy Skunk had played him a mean trick and for a few minutes he was very mad. But Jimmy Skunk soon told him who had filled up his doorway with the big stone.

"Now you push from that side, Johnny Chuck, and I'll pull from this side, and we'll soon have this big stone out of your doorway," said Jimmy Skunk.

So Johnny Chuck pushed and Jimmy Skunk pulled, and sure enough they soon had the big stone out of Johnny Chuck's doorway.

"Now," said Jimmy Skunk, "we'll roll this big stone down the Lone Little Path to Reddy Fox's house and we'll give Reddy Fox a surprise."

So Johnny Chuck and Jimmy Skunk tugged and pulled and rolled the big stone down to the house of Reddy Fox, and sure enough, it filled his doorway.

"Good night, Jimmy Skunk," said Johnny Chuck, and trotted down the Lone Little Path toward home, chuckling to himself all the way.

Jimmy Skunk walked slowly up the Lone Little Path to the wood, for Jimmy Skunk never hurries. Pretty soon he came to the big hollow tree where Bobby Coon lives, and there he met Hooty the Owl.

"Hello, Jimmy Skunk, where have you been?" asked Hooty the Owl.

"Just for a walk," said Jimmy Skunk. "Who lives in this big hollow tree?"

Now of course Jimmy Skunk knew all the time, but he pretended he didn't.

"Oh, this is Bobby Coon's house," said Hooty the Owl.

"Let's give Bobby Coon a surprise," said Jimmy Skunk.

"How?" asked Hooty the Owl.

"We'll fill his house full of sticks and leaves," said Jimmy Skunk.

Hooty the Owl thought that would be a good joke, so while Jimmy Skunk gathered all the old sticks and leaves he could find, Hooty the Owl stuffed them into the old hollow tree which was Bobby Coon's house, until he couldn't get in another one.

"Good night," said Jimmy Skunk as he began to climb the Crooked Little Path up the hill to his own snug little home.

"Good night," said Hooty the Owl, as he flew like a big soft shadow over to the Great Pine.

By and by when old Mother Moon was just going to bed and all the little stars were too sleepy to twinkle any longer, Reddy Fox and Bobby Coon, very tired and very wet from playing in the Laughing Brook, came up the Lone Little Path, ready to tumble into their snug little beds. They were chuckling over the trick they had played on Johnny Chuck, and the way they had waked up old Grandfather Frog, and all the other mischief they had done. What do you suppose they said when they reached their homes and found that someone else had been playing jokes, too?

I'm sure I don't know, but round, red Mr. Sun was laughing very hard as he peeped over the hill at Reddy Fox and Bobby Coon, and he won't tell why.

CHAPTER XIII

~

JOHNNY CHUCK FINDS THE BEST THING IN THE WORLD

Old Mother West Wind had stopped to talk with the Slender Fir Tree.

"I've just come across the Green Meadows," said Old Mother West Wind, "and there I saw the Best Thing in the World."

Striped Chipmunk was sitting under the Slender Fir Tree and he couldn't help hearing what Old Mother West Wind said. "The Best Thing in the World—now what can that be?" thought Striped Chipmunk. "Why, it must be heaps and heaps of nuts and acorns! I'll go and find it."

So Striped Chipmunk started down the Lone Little Path through the wood as fast as he could run. Pretty soon he met Peter Rabbit.

"Where are you going in such a hurry, Striped Chipmunk?" asked Peter Rabbit.

"Down in the Green Meadows to find the Best Thing in the World," replied Striped Chipmunk, and ran faster.

"The Best Thing in the World," said Peter Rabbit, "why, that must be great piles of carrots and cabbage! I think I'll go and find it."

So Peter Rabbit started down the Lone Little Path through the wood as fast as he could go after Striped Chipmunk.

As they passed the great hollow tree Bobby Coon put his head out. "Where are you going in such a hurry?" asked Bobby Coon.

"Down in the Green Meadows to find the Best Thing in the World!" shouted Striped Chipmunk and Peter Rabbit, and both began to run faster.

"The Best Thing in the World," said Bobby Coon to himself. "Why, that must be a whole

"Where are you going in such a hurry, Striped
Chipmunk?" asked Peter Rabbit. *Page 94.*

field of sweet milky corn. I think I'll go and find it."

So Bobby Coon climbed down out of the great hollow tree and started down the Lone Little Path through the wood as fast as he could go after Striped Chipmunk and Peter Rabbit, for there is nothing that Bobby Coon likes to eat so well as sweet milky corn.

At the edge of the wood they met Jimmy Skunk.

"Where are you going in such a hurry?" asked Jimmy Skunk.

"Down in the Green Meadows to find the Best Thing in the World!" shouted Striped Chipmunk and Peter Rabbit and Bobby Coon. Then they all tried to run faster.

"The Best Thing in the World," said Jimmy Skunk. "Why, that must be packs and packs of beetles!" And for once in his life Jimmy Skunk began to hurry down the Lone Little Path after Striped Chipmunk and Peter Rabbit and Bobby Coon.

They were all running so fast that they didn't see Reddy Fox until he jumped out of the long grass and asked:

"Where are you going in such a hurry?"

"To find the Best Thing in the World!" shouted Striped Chipmunk and Peter Rabbit and Bobby Coon and Jimmy Skunk, and each did his best to run faster.

"The Best Thing in the World," said Reddy Fox to himself. "Why, that must be a whole pen full of tender young chickens, and I must have them."

So away went Reddy Fox as fast as he could run down the Lone Little Path after Striped Chipmunk, Peter Rabbit, Bobby Coon and Jimmy Skunk.

By and by they all came to the house of Johnny Chuck.

"Where are you going in such a hurry?" asked Johnny Chuck.

"To find the Best Thing in the World," shouted Striped Chipmunk and Peter Rabbit and Bobby Coon and Jimmy Skunk and Reddy Fox.

"The Best Thing in the World," said Johnny Chuck. "Why, I don't know of anything better than my own little home and the warm sunshine and the beautiful blue sky."

So Johnny Chuck stayed at home and played all day among the flowers with the Merry Little Breezes of Old Mother West Wind and was as happy as could be.

But all day long Striped Chipmunk and Peter Rabbit and Bobby Coon and Jimmy Skunk and Reddy Fox ran this way and ran that way over the Green Meadows trying to find the Best Thing in the World. The sun was very, very warm and they ran so far and they ran so fast that they were very, very hot and tired, and still they hadn't found the Best Thing in the World.

When the long day was over they started up the Lone Little Path past Johnny Chuck's house to their own homes. They didn't hurry now for they were so very, very tired! And they were cross—oh so cross! Striped Chipmunk hadn't found a single nut. Peter Rabbit hadn't found so much as the leaf of a cabbage. Bobby Coon hadn't found

"Johnny Chuck has it," said Old
Mother West Wind. *Page 100.*

the tiniest bit of sweet milky corn. Jimmy Skunk hadn't seen a single beetle. Reddy Fox hadn't heard so much as the peep of a chicken. And all were as hungry as hungry could be.

Half way up the Lone Little Path they met Old Mother West Wind going to her home behind the hill. "Did you find the Best Thing in the World?" asked Old Mother West Wind.

"No!" shouted Striped Chipmunk and Peter Rabbit and Bobby Coon and Jimmy Skunk and Reddy Fox all together.

"Johnny Chuck has it," said Old Mother West Wind. "It is being happy with the things you have and not wanting things which some one else has. And it is called Con-tent-ment."

CHAPTER XIV

~

LITTLE JOE OTTER'S SLIPPERY SLIDE

Little Joe Otter and Billy Mink had been playing together around the Smiling Pool all one sunshiny morning. They had been fishing and had taken home a fine dinner of Trout for old Grandfather Mink and blind old Granny Otter. They had played tag with the Merry Little Breezes. They had been in all kinds of mischief and now they just didn't know what to do.

They were sitting side by side on the Big Rock trying to push each other off into the Smiling Pool. Round, smiling, red Mr. Sun made the Green Meadows very warm indeed, and Reddy Fox, over in the tall grass, heard them splashing and shouting and having such a good time that he wished he liked the nice cool water and could swim, too.

"I've thought of something!" cried Little Joe Otter.

"What is it?" asked Billy Mink.

Little Joe Otter just looked wise and said nothing.

"Something to eat?" asked Billy Mink.

"No," said Little Joe Otter.

"I don't believe you've a thought of anything at all," said Billy Mink.

"I have too!" said Little Joe Otter. "It's something to do."

"What?" demanded Billy Mink.

Just then Little Joe Otter spied Jerry Muskrat. "Hi, Jerry Muskrat! Come over here!" he called.

Jerry Muskrat swam across to the Big Rock and climbed up beside Billy Mink and Little Joe Otter.

"What are you fellows doing?" asked Jerry Muskrat.

"Having some fun," said Billy Mink. "Little Joe Otter has thought of something to do, but I don't know what it is."

"Let's make a slide," cried Little Joe Otter.

"You show us how," said Billy Mink.

So Little Joe Otter found a nice smooth place on the bank, and Billy Mink and Jerry Muskrat brought mud and helped him pat it down smooth until they had the loveliest slippery slide in the world. Then Little Joe Otter climbed up the bank to the top of the slippery slide and lay down flat on his stomach. Billy Mink gave a push and away he went down, down the slippery slide, splash into the Smiling Pool. Then Jerry Muskrat tried it and after him Billy Mink. Then all did it over again. Sometimes they went down the slippery slide on their backs, sometimes flat on their stomachs, sometimes head first, sometimes feet first. Oh such fun as they did have! Even Grandfather Frog came over and tried the slippery slide.

Johnny Chuck, over in the Green Meadows, heard the noise and stole down the Lone Little

Path to see. Jimmy Skunk, looking for beetles up on the hill, heard the noise and forgot that he hadn't had his breakfast. Reddy Fox, taking a nap, woke up and hurried over to watch the fun. Last of all came Peter Rabbit.

Little Joe Otter saw him coming. "Hello, Peter Rabbit!" he shouted. "Come and try the slippery slide."

Now Peter Rabbit couldn't swim, but he pretended that he didn't want to.

"I've left my bathing suit at home," said Peter Rabbit.

"Never mind," said Billy Mink. "Mr. Sun will dry you off."

"And we'll help," said all the Merry Little Breezes of Old Mother West Wind.

But Peter Rabbit shook his head and said, "No."

Faster and faster went Billy Mink and Little Joe Otter and Jerry Muskrat and old Grandfather Frog down the slippery slide into the Smiling Pool.

Peter Rabbit kept coming near and nearer until finally he stood right at the top of the slippery slide. Billy Mink crept up behind him very softly and gave him a push. Peter Rabbit's long legs flew out from under him and down he sat with a thump on the slippery slide. "Oh," cried Peter Rabbit, and tried to stop himself. But he couldn't do it and so away he went down the slippery slide, splash into the Smiling Pool.

"Ha! ha! ha!" laughed Billy Mink.

"Ho! ho! ho!" shouted Little Joe Otter.

"He! he! he!" laughed Jerry Muskrat and old Grandfather Frog and Sammy Jay and Jimmy Skunk and Reddy Fox and Blacky the Crow and Mr. Kingfisher, for you know Peter Rabbit was forever playing jokes on them.

Poor Peter Rabbit! The water got in his eyes and up his nose and into his mouth and made him choke and splutter, and then he couldn't get back on the bank, for you know Peter Rabbit couldn't swim.

Away he went down the slippery slide. *Page 105.*

When Little Joe Otter saw what a dreadful time Peter Rabbit was having he dove into the Smiling Pool and took hold of one of Peter Rabbit's long ears. Billy Mink swam out and took hold of the other long ear. Jerry Muskrat swam right under Peter Rabbit and took him on his back. Then with old Grandfather Frog swimming ahead they took Peter Rabbit right across the Smiling Pool and pulled him out on the grassy bank, where it was nice and warm. All the Merry Little Breezes of Old Mother West Wind came over and helped Mr. Sun dry Peter Rabbit off.

Then they all sat down together and watched Little Joe Otter turn a somersault down the slippery slide.

CHAPTER XV

~

THE TALE OF TOMMY TROUT WHO DIDN'T MIND

In the Laughing Brook, which ripples and sings all day long, lived Mr. Trout and Mrs. Trout, and a whole lot of little Trouts. There were so many little Trouts that Mr. Trout and Mrs. Trout were kept very busy indeed getting breakfast and dinner and supper for them, and watching out for them and teaching them how to swim and how to catch foolish little flies that sometimes fell on the water and how to keep out of the way of big hungry fish and sharp eyed Mr. Kingfisher and big men and little boys who came fishing with hooks and lines.

Now all the little Trouts were very, very good and minded just what Mrs. Trout told them—all but Tommy Trout, for Tommy Trout—oh, dear, dear! Tommy Trout never could mind right away. He always had to wait a little instead of minding when he was spoken to.

Tommy Trout didn't mean to be bad. Oh dear, no! He just wanted to have his own way, and because Tommy Trout had his own way and didn't mind Mrs. Trout there isn't any Tommy Trout now. No sir, there isn't as much as one little blue spot of his beautiful little coat left because—why, just because Tommy Trout didn't mind.

One day when round, red Mr. Sun was shining and the Laughing Brook was singing on its way to join the Big River, Mrs. Trout started out to get some nice plump flies for dinner. All the little Trouts were playing in their dear little pool, safe behind the Big Rock. Before she started Mrs. Trout called all the little Trouts around her and told them not to leave their little pool while she was gone, "For," said she, "something dreadful might happen to you."

Mrs. Trout started out to get some nice
plump flies for dinner. *Page 110.*

All the little Trouts, except Tommy Trout, promised that they would surely, surely stay inside their dear little pool. Then they all began to jump and chase each other and play as happy as could be, all but Tommy Trout.

As soon as Mrs. Trout had started, Tommy Trout swam off by himself to the edge of the pool. "I wonder what is on the other side of the Big Rock," said Tommy Trout. "The sun is shining and the brook is laughing and nothing could happen if I go just a little speck of a ways."

So, when no one was looking, Tommy Trout slipped out of the safe little pool where all the other little Trouts were playing. He swam just a little speck of a ways farther still. Now he could see almost around the Big Rock. Then he swam just a little speck of a ways farther and—oh dear, dear! he looked right into the mouth of a great big, big fish called Mr. Pickerel, who is very fond of little Trouts and would like to eat one for breakfast every day.

"Ah ha!" said Mr. Pickerel, opening his big, big mouth very, very wide.

Tommy Trout turned to run back to the dear, dear safe little pool where all the other little Trouts were playing so happily, but he was too late. Into that great big, big mouth he went instead, and Mr. Pickerel swallowed him whole.

"Ah ha," said Mr. Pickerel, "I like little Trouts."

And nothing more was ever heard of Tommy Trout, who didn't mind.

CHAPTER XVI

~

SPOTTY THE TURTLE WINS A RACE

All the little people who live on the Green Meadows and in the Smiling Pool and along the Laughing Brook were to have a holiday. The Merry Little Breezes of Old Mother West Wind had been very busy, oh very busy indeed, in sending word to all the little meadow folks. You see, Peter Rabbit had been boasting of how fast he could run. Reddy Fox was quite sure that he could run faster than Peter Rabbit. Billy Mink, who can move so quickly you hardly can see him, was quite sure that neither Peter Rabbit nor Reddy Fox could run as fast as he. They all met one day beside the Smiling Pool and agreed that old Grandfather Frog should decide who was the swiftest.

Now Grandfather Frog was accounted very wise. You see he had lived a long time, oh, very much longer than any of the others, and therefore, because of the wisdom of age, Grandfather Frog was always called on to decide all disputes. He sat on his green lily-pad while Billy Mink sat on the Big Rock, and Peter Rabbit and Reddy Fox sat on the bank. Each in turn told why he thought he was the fastest. Old Grandfather Frog listened and listened and said never a word until they were all through. When they had finished, he stopped to catch a foolish green fly and then he said:

"The best way to decide who is the swiftest is to have a race."

So it was agreed that Peter Rabbit and Reddy Fox and Billy Mink should start together from the old butternut tree on one edge of the Green Meadows, race away across the Green Meadows to the little hill on the other side and each bring back a nut from the big hickory which grew there. The one who first reached the old butter-nut tree with a hickory nut would be declared the winner. The Merry Little Breezes flew about over the Green Meadows telling everyone about the race and everyone planned to be there.

It was a beautiful summer day. Mr. Sun smiled and smiled, and the more he smiled the warmer it grew. Everyone was there to see the race—Striped Chipmunk, Happy Jack Squirrel, Sammy Jay, Blacky the Crow, Hooty the Owl and Bobby Coon all sat up in the old butternut tree where it was cool and shady. Johnny Chuck, Jerry Muskrat, Jimmy Skunk, Little Joe Otter, Grandfather Frog and even old Mr. Toad, were there. Last of all came Spotty the Turtle. Now Spotty the Turtle is a very slow walker, and he cannot run at all. When Peter Rabbit saw him coming up towards the old butternut tree he shouted: "Come, Spotty, don't you want to race with us?"

Everybody laughed because you know Spotty is so very, very slow; but Spotty didn't laugh and he didn't get cross because everyone else laughed.

"There is a wise old saying, Peter Rabbit," said Spotty the Turtle, "which shows that those who run fastest do not always reach a place first. I think I *will* enter this race."

Every one thought that that was the best joke they had heard for a long time, and all laughed harder than ever. They all agreed that Spotty the Turtle should start in the race too.

So they all stood in a row, Peter Rabbit first, then Billy Mink, then Reddy Fox, and right side of Reddy Fox Spotty the Turtle.

"Are you ready?" asked Grandfather Frog. "Go!"

Away went Peter Rabbit with great big jumps. After him went Billy Mink so fast that was just a little brown streak going through the tall grass, and side by side with him ran Reddy Fox. Now just as they started Spotty the Turtle reached up and grabbed the long hair on the end of Reddy's big tail. Of course Reddy couldn't have stopped to shake him off, because Peter Rabbit and Billy Mink were running so fast that he had to run his very best to keep up with them. But he didn't even know that Spotty the Turtle was there. You see Spotty is not very heavy and Reddy Fox was so excited that he did not notice that his big tail was heavier than usual.

The Merry Little Breezes flew along, too, to see that the race was fair. Peter Rabbit went with great big jumps. Whenever he came to a little bush he jumped right over it, for Peter Rabbit's legs are long and meant for jumping. Billy Mink is so slim that he slipped between the bushes and through the long grass like a little brown streak. Reddy Fox, who is bigger than either Peter Rabbit or Billy Mink, had no trouble in keeping up with them. Not one of them noticed that Spotty the Turtle was hanging fast to the end of Reddy's tail.

Now just at the foot of the little hill on which the big hickory tree grew was a little pond. It wasn't very wide but it was quite long. Billy Mink remembered this pond and he chuckled to himself as he raced along, for he knew that Peter Rabbit couldn't swim and he knew that Reddy Fox does not like the water, so therefore both would have to run around it. He himself can swim even faster than he can run. The more he thought of this, the more foolish it seemed that he should hurry so on such a warm day. "For," said Billy Mink to himself, "even if they reach the pond first, they will have to run around it, while I can swim across it and cool off while I am swimming. I will surely get there first." So Billy Mink ran slower and slower, and pretty soon he had dropped behind.

Mr. Sun, round and red, looking down, smiled and smiled to see the race. The more he smiled the warmer it grew. Now, Peter Rabbit had a thick gray coat and Reddy Fox had a thick red coat, and they both began to get very, very warm. Peter Rabbit did not make such long jumps as when he first started. Reddy Fox began to feel very thirsty, and his tongue hung out. Now that Billy Mink was behind them they thought they did not need to hurry so.

Peter Rabbit reached the little pond first. He had not thought of that pond when he agreed to enter the race. He stopped right on the edge of it and sat up on his hind legs. Right across he could see the big hickory tree, so near and yet so far, for he knew that he must run around the pond then back again, and it was a long, long way. In just a moment Reddy Fox ran out of the bushes and Reddy felt much as Peter Rabbit did. Way, way behind them was Billy Mink, trotting along comfortably and chuckling to himself. Peter Rabbit looked at Reddy Fox in dismay, and Reddy Fox looked at Peter Rabbit in dismay. Then they both looked at Billy Mink and remembered that Billy Mink could swim right across.

Then off Peter Rabbit started as fast as he could go around the pond one way, and Reddy Fox started around the pond the other way. They were so excited that neither noticed a little splash in the pond. That was Spotty the Turtle who had let go of Reddy's tail and now was swimming across the pond, for you know that Spotty is a splendid swimmer. Only once or twice he stuck his little black nose up to get some air. The rest of the time he swam under water and no one but the Merry Little Breezes saw him. Right across he swam, and climbed up the bank right under the big hickory tree.

Now there were just three nuts left under the hickory trees. Two of these Spotty took down to the edge of the pond and buried in the mud. The other he took in his mouth and started back across the pond. Just as he reached the other shore up trotted Billy Mink, but Billy Mink didn't see Spotty. He was too intent watching Reddy Fox and Peter Rabbit, who were now half way around the pond. In he jumped with a splash. My! How good that cool water did feel! He didn't have to hurry now, because he felt sure that the race was his. So he swam round and round and chased some fish and had a beautiful time in the water. By and by he looked up and saw that Peter Rabbit was almost around the pond one way and Reddy Fox was almost around the pond the other way. They both looked tired and hot and discouraged.

Then Billy Mink swam slowly across and climbed out on the bank under the big hickory tree. But where were the nuts? Look as he would, he could not see a nut anywhere, yet the Merry Little Breezes had said there were three nuts lying under the hickory tree. Billy Mink ran this way and ran that way. He was still running around, poking over the leaves and looking under the twigs and pieces of bark when Peter Rabbit and Reddy Fox came up.

Then they, too, began to look under the leaves and under the bark. They pawed around in the grass, they hunted in every nook and cranny, but not a nut could they find. They were tired and cross and hot and they accused Billy Mink of having hidden the nuts. Billy Mink stoutly insisted that he had not hidden the nuts, that he had not found the nuts, and when they saw how hard he was hunting they believed him.

All the afternoon they hunted and hunted and hunted, and all the afternoon Spotty the Turtle, with the nut in his mouth, was slowly, oh, so slowly, crawling straight back across the Green Meadows towards the old butternut tree. Round, red Mr. Sun was getting very close to the Purple Hills, where he goes to bed every night, and all the little meadow folks were getting ready to go to their homes. They were wondering and wondering what could have happened to the racers, when Sammy Jay spied the Merry Little Breezes dancing across the Green Meadows.

"Here come the Merry Little Breezes; they'll tell us who wins the race," cried Sammy Jay.

When the Merry Little Breezes reached the old butternut tree, all the little meadow folks crowded around them, but the Merry Little Breezes just laughed and laughed and wouldn't say a word. Then all of a sudden, out of the tall meadow grass crept Spotty the Turtle and laid the hickory nut at the feet of old Grandfather Frog. Old Grandfather Frog was so surprised that he actually let a great green fly buzz right past his nose.

"Where did you get that hickory nut?" asked Grandfather Frog.

"Under the big hickory tree on the hill on the other side of the Green Meadows," said Spotty.

Then all the Merry Little Breezes clapped their hands and shouted: "He did! He did! Spotty wins the race!"

Then they told how Spotty reached the pond by clinging to the tip of Reddy Fox's tail, and had hidden the other two nuts, and then how he had patiently crawled home while Billy Mink and Reddy Fox and Peter Rabbit were hunting and hunting and hunting for the nuts they could not find.

And so Spotty the Turtle was awarded the race, and to this day Peter Rabbit and Reddy Fox and Billy Mink can't bear the sight of a hickory nut.

THE END

MOTHER WEST WIND'S CHILDREN

by

THORNTON W. BURGESS

To
all the little friends
of Johnny Chuck and Reddy Fox,
and to
all who love the Green Meadows
and the Smiling Pool,
the Laughing Brook and the Merry Little Breezes,
this little book is dedicated.

"Yap-yap-yap," barked Reddy Fox, as loud as he could." *Page 173.*

CHAPTER I

~

DANNY MEADOW MOUSE LEARNS WHY HIS TAIL IS SHORT

Danny Meadow Mouse sat in his doorway and looked down the Lone Little Path across the Green Meadows. Way, way over near the Smiling Pool he could see Old Mother West Wind's Children, the Merry Little Breezes, at play. Sammy Jay was sitting on a fence post. He pretended to be taking a sun bath, but really he was planning mischief. You never see Sammy Jay that he isn't in mischief or planning it.

Reddy Fox had trotted past an hour before in a great hurry. Up on the hill Danny Meadow

Mouse could just see Jimmy Skunk pulling over every old stick and stone he could find, no matter whose house it might be, and excusing himself because he was hungry and was looking for beetles.

Jolly, round, red Mr. Sun was playing at hide and seek behind some fleecy white clouds. All the birds were singing and singing, and the world was happy—all but Danny Meadow Mouse.

No, Danny Meadow Mouse was not happy. Indeed, he was very far from happy, and all because his tail was short.

By and by up came old Mr. Toad. It was a warm day and Mr. Toad was very hot and very, very thirsty. He stopped to rest beside the house of Danny Meadow Mouse.

"Good morning, Danny Meadow Mouse," said old Mr. Toad, "it's a fine morning."

"Morning," said Danny Meadow Mouse, grumpily.

"I hope your health is good this morning," continued old Mr. Toad, just as if he hadn't noticed how short and cross Danny Meadow Mouse had answered.

Now old Mr. Toad is very ugly to look upon, but the ugliness is all in his looks. He has the sunniest of hearts and always he is looking for a chance to help someone.

"Danny Meadow Mouse," said old Mr. Toad, "you make me think of your grandfather a thousand times removed. You do indeed. You look just as he did when he lost the half of his tail and realized that he never, never could get it back again."

Danny Meadow Mouse sat up suddenly.

"What are you talking about, old Mr. Toad? What are you talking about?" he asked. "Did my grandfather a thousand times removed lose the half of his tail, and was it shorter then than mine is now? Was it, old Mr. Toad? And how did he come to lose the half of it?"

Old Mr. Toad laughed a funny silent laugh. "It's a long story," said old Mr. Toad, and I'm afraid I can't tell it. Go down to the Smiling Pool and ask Great-Grandfather Frog, who is my first cousin, how it happened your grandfather a thousand times removed lost the half of his tail. But before you go catch three fat, foolish, green flies and take them with you as a present to Grandfather Frog."

Danny Meadow Mouse could hardly wait for old Mr. Toad to stop speaking. In fact, he was in such a hurry that he almost forgot his manners. Not quite, however, for he shouted "Thank you, Mr. Toad, thank you!" over his shoulder as he rushed off down the Lone Little Path.

You see his short tail had always been a matter of mortification to Danny Meadow Mouse. All his cousins in the Mouse family and the Rat family have long, smooth, tapering tails, and they have always been a source of envy to Danny Meadow Mouse. He had felt his queer short tail to be a sort of disgrace. So when he would meet one of his cousins dancing down the Lone Little Path, with his long, slim, tapering tail behind him, Danny Meadow Mouse would slip out of sight under the long grass, he was so ashamed of his own little tail. It looked so mean and small! He had wondered and wondered if the Meadow Mice had always had short tails. He used to ask everyone who came his way if they had ever seen a Meadow Mouse with a long tail, but he had never found any one who had.

"Perhaps," thought Danny Meadow Mouse as he hurried down the Lone Little Path, "perhaps Grandfather Frog, who is very wise, will know why my tail is short."

So he hurried this way and he hurried that way over the Green Meadows in search of fat, foolish, green flies. And when he had caught three, he caught one more for good measure. Then he started for the Smiling Pool as fast as his short legs would take him.

When finally he reached the edge of the Smiling Pool he was quite out of breath. There sat Great-Grandfather Frog on his big, green lily pad. He was blinking his great goggle eyes at jolly, round, red Mr. Sun.

"Oh, Grandfather Frog," said Danny Meadow Mouse in a very small voice, for you know he was quite out of breath with running, "Oh, Grandfather Frog, I've brought you four fat, foolish, green flies."

Grandfather Frog put a hand behind an ear and listened. "Did I hear someone say 'foolish, green flies?'" asked Grandfather Frog.

"Yes, Grandfather Frog, here they are," said Danny Meadow Mouse, still in a very small voice. Then he gave Grandfather Frog the four fat, foolish, green flies.

"What is it that you want me to do for you, Danny Meadow Mouse?" asked Grandfather Frog as he smacked his lips, for he knew that Danny Meadow Mouse must want something to bring him four fat, foolish, green flies.

"If you please," said Danny Meadow Mouse, very politely, "if you please, Grandfather Frog, old Mr. Toad told me that you could tell me how Grandfather Meadow Mouse a thousand times removed lost half of his tail. Will you, Grandfather Frog—will you?"

"Chug-a-rum," said Grandfather Frog. "My cousin, Mr. Toad, talks too much."

But he settled himself comfortably on the big lily pad, and this is what he told Danny Meadow Mouse:

"Once upon a time, when the world was young, Mr. Meadow Mouse, your grandfather a thousand times removed, was a very fine gentleman. He took a great deal of pride in his appearance, did Mr. Meadow Mouse, and they used to say on the Green Meadows that he spent an hour, a full hour, every day combing his whiskers and brushing his coat.

"Anyway, he was very fine to look upon, was Mr. Meadow Mouse, and not the least attractive thing about him was his beautiful, long, slim tail, of which he was very proud.

"Now about this time there was a great deal of trouble on the Green Meadows and in the Green Forest, for some one was stealing—yes, stealing! Mr. Rabbit complained first. To be sure, Mr. Rabbit was lazy and his cabbage patch had grown little more than weeds while he had been minding other folks' affairs rather than his own, but, then, that was no reason why he should lose half of the little which he did raise. And that is just what he said had happened.

"No one really believed what Mr. Rabbit said, for he had such a bad name for telling things which were not so that when he did tell the truth no one could be quite sure of it.

"So no one paid much heed to what Mr. Rabbit said until Happy Jack Squirrel one day went to his snug little hollow in the big chestnut tree where he stores his nuts and discovered half had been stolen. Then Striped Chipmunk lost the greater part of his winter store of corn. A fat trout was stolen from Billy Mink.

"It was a terrible time, for every one suspected every one else, and no one on the Green Meadows was happy.

"One evening Mr. Meadow Mouse went for a stroll along the Crooked Little Path up the hill. It was dark, very dark indeed. But just as he passed Striped Chipmunk's granary, the place where he stores his supply of corn and acorns for the winter, Mr. Meadow Mouse met his cousin, Mr. Wharf Rat. Now Mr. Wharf Rat was very big and strong and Mr. Meadow Mouse had for a long time looked up to and admired him.

"'Good evening, Cousin Meadow Mouse,' said Mr. Wharf Rat, swinging a bag down from his shoulder. 'Will you do a favor for me?'

"Now Mr. Meadow Mouse felt very much flattered, and as he was a very obliging fellow anyway, he promptly said he would.

"'All right,' said Mr. Wharf Rat. 'I'm going to get you to tote this bag down the Crooked Little Path to the hollow chestnut tree. I've got an errand back on top of the hill.'

"So Mr. Meadow Mouse picked up the bag, which was very heavy, and swung it over his shoulder. Then he started down the Crooked Little Path. Half way down he met Striped Chipmunk.

"'Good evening, Mr. Meadow Mouse,' said Striped Chipmunk. 'What are you toting in the bag across your shoulder?'

"Now, of course, Mr. Meadow Mouse didn't know what was in the bag and he didn't like to admit that he was working for another, for he was very proud, was Mr. Meadow Mouse.

"So he said: 'Just a planting of potatoes I begged from Jimmy Skunk, just a planting of potatoes, Striped Chipmunk.'

"Now no one had ever suspected Mr. Meadow Mouse of stealing—no indeed! Striped Chipmunk would have gone his way and thought no more about it, had it not happened that there was a hole in the bag and from it something dropped at his feet. Striped Chipmunk picked it up and it *wasn't* a potato. It was a fat acorn. Striped Chipmunk said nothing but slipped it into his pocket.

"'Good night,' said Mr. Meadow Mouse, once more shouldering the bag.

"'Good night,' said Striped Chipmunk.

"No sooner had Mr. Meadow Mouse disappeared in the darkness down the Crooked Little Path than Striped Chipmunk hurried to his granary. Some one had been there and stolen all his acorns!

"Then Striped Chipmunk ran to the house of his cousin, Happy Jack Squirrel, and told him how the acorns had been stolen from his granary and how he had met Mr. Meadow Mouse with a bag over his shoulder and how Mr. Meadow Mouse had said that he was toting home a planting of potatoes he had begged from Jimmy Skunk. 'And this,' said Striped Chipmunk, holding out the fat acorn, 'is what fell out of the bag.'

"Then Striped Chipmunk and Happy Jack Squirrel hurried over to Jimmy Skunk's house, and, just as they expected, they found that Mr. Meadow Mouse had not begged a planting of potatoes of Jimmy Skunk.

"So Striped Chipmunk and Happy Jack Squirrel and Jimmy Skunk hurried over to Mr. Rabbit's and told him all about Mr. Meadow Mouse and the bag of potatoes that dropped acorns. Mr. Rabbit looked very grave, very grave indeed. Then Striped Chipmunk and Happy Jack Squirrel and Jimmy Skunk and Mr. Rabbit started to tell Mr. Coon, who was cousin to old King Bear.

"On the way they met Hooty the Owl, and because he could fly softly and quickly, they sent Hooty the Owl to tell all the meadow people who were awake to come to the hollow chestnut tree. So Hooty the Owl flew away to tell all the little meadow people who were awake to meet at the hollow chestnut tree.

"When they reached the hollow chestnut tree whom should they find there but Mr. Meadow Mouse fast asleep beside the bag he had brought for Mr. Wharf Rat, who had wisely stayed away.

"Very softly Striped Chipmunk stole up and opened the bag. Out fell his store of fat acorns. Then they waked Mr. Meadow Mouse and marched him off to old Mother Nature, where they charged him with being a thief.

"Old Mother Nature listened to all they had to say. She saw the bag of acorns and she heard how Mr. Meadow Mouse had said that he had a planting of potatoes. Then she asked him if he had stolen the acorns. Yes, Sir, she asked him right out if he had stolen the acorns.

"Of course Mr. Meadow Mouse said that he had not stolen the acorns.

"'Then where did you get the bag of acorns?' asked old Mother Nature.

"When she asked this, Mr. Wharf Rat, who was sitting in the crowd of meadow people, got up and softly tiptoed away when he thought no one was looking. But old Mother Nature saw him. You can't fool old Mother Nature. No, Sir, you can't fool old Mother Nature, and it's of no use to try.

"Mr. Meadow Mouse didn't know what to say. He knew now that Mr. Wharf Rat must be the thief, but Mr. Wharf Rat was his cousin, and he had always looked up to him as a very fine gentleman. He couldn't tell the world that Mr. Wharf Rat was a thief. So Mr. Meadow Mouse said nothing.

"Three times old Mother Nature asked Mr. Meadow Mouse where he got the bag of acorns, and each time Mr. Meadow Mouse said nothing.

"'Mr. Meadow Mouse,' said old Mother Nature, and her voice was very stern, 'I know that you did not steal the acorns of Striped Chipmunk. I know that you did not even guess that there were stolen acorns in that bag. Everyone else thinks that you are the thief who caused so much trouble on the Green Meadows and in the Green Forest. But I know who the real thief is and he is stealing away as fast as he can go down the Lone Little Path this very minute.'

"All of the little meadow people and forest folks turned to look down the Lone Little Path, but it was so dark none could see, none but Hooty the Owl, whose eyes are made to see in the dark.

"'I see him!' cried Hooty the Owl. 'It's Mr. Wharf Rat!'

"'Yes,' said old Mother Nature, 'it's Mr. Wharf Rat—he is the thief. And this shall be his punishment: Always hereafter he will be driven out wherever he is found. He shall no longer live in the Green Meadows or the Green Forest. Everyone will turn their backs upon him. He will live on what others throw away. He will live in filth and there will be no one to say a good word for him. He will become an outcast instead of a fine gentleman.'

"'And you, Mr. Meadow Mouse, in order that you may remember always to avoid bad company, and that while it is a splendid thing to be loyal to your friends and not to tell tales, it is also a very, very wrong thing to shield those who have done wrong when by so doing you simply help them to keep on doing wrong—you shall no longer have the splendid long tail of which you are so proud, but it shall be short and stubby.'

"Even while old Mother Nature was speaking, Mr. Meadow Mouse felt his tail grow shorter and shorter, and when she had finished he had just a little mean stub of a tail.

"Of course he felt terribly. And while Striped Chipmunk hurried to tell him how sorry he felt, and while all the other little meadow people also hurried to tell him how sorry they felt, he could not be comforted. So he slipped away as quickly as he could, and because he was so ashamed he crept along underneath the long grass that no one should see his short tail. And ever since that long ago time when the world was young," concluded Grandfather Frog, "the Meadow Mice have had short tails and have always scurried along under cover of the long grass where no one will see them. And the Wharf Rats have never again lived in the Green Meadows or in the Green Forest, but have lived on filth and garbage around the homes of men, with every man's hand against them."

"Thank you, Grandfather Frog," said Danny Meadow Mouse, very soberly. "Now I understand why my tail is short and I shall not forget."

"But it isn't your fault at all, Danny Meadow Mouse," cried the Merry Little Breezes, who had been listening, "and we love you just as much as if your tail was long!"

Then they played tag with him all the way up the Lone Little Path to his house, till Danny Meadow Mouse quite forgot that he had wished that his tail was long.

CHAPTER II

~

WHY REDDY FOX HAS NO FRIENDS

The Green Meadows lay peaceful and still. Mother Moon, sailing high overhead, looked down upon them and smiled and smiled, flooding them with her silvery light. All day long the Merry Little Breezes of Old Mother West Wind had romped there among the asters and goldenrod. They had played tag through the cat rushes around the Smiling Pool. For very mischief they had rubbed the fur of the Field Mice babies the wrong way and had blown a fat green fly right out of Grandfather Frog's mouth just as his lips came together with a smack. Now they were safely tucked in bed behind the Purple Hills, and so they missed the midnight feast at the foot of the Lone Pine.

But Reddy Fox was there. You can always count on Reddy Fox to be about when mischief or good times are afoot, especially after Mr. Sun has pulled his nightcap on.

Jimmy Skunk was there. If there is any mischief Reddy Fox does not think of Jimmy Skunk will be sure to discover it.

Billy Mink was there. Yes indeed, Billy Mink was there! Billy Mink is another mischief maker. When Reddy Fox and Jimmy Skunk are playing pranks or in trouble of any kind you are certain to find Billy Mink close by. That is, you are certain to find him if you look sharp enough. But Billy Mink is so slim, he moves so quickly, and his wits are so sharp, that he is not seen half so often as the others.

With Billy Mink came his cousin, Shadow the Weasel, who is sly and cruel. No one likes Shadow the Weasel.

Little Joe Otter and Jerry Muskrat came. They were late, for the legs of Little Joe Otter are so short that he is a slow traveler on land, while Jerry Muskrat feels much more at home in the water than on the dry ground.

Of course Peter Rabbit was there. Without him no party on the Green Meadows would be complete, and Peter likes to be abroad at night even better than by day. With Peter came his cousin, Jumper the Hare, who had come down from the Pine Forest for a visit.

Boomer the Nighthawk and Hooty the Owl completed the party, though Hooty had not been invited and no one knew that he was there.

Each was to contribute something to the feast—the thing that he liked best. Such an array as Mother Moon looked down upon! Reddy Fox had brought a plump, tender chicken, stolen from Farmer Brown's dooryard.

Very quietly, like a thin, brown shadow, Billy Mink had slipped up to the duck pond and— alas! Now Mother Quack had one less in her pretty little flock than when as jolly, round, red Mr. Sun went to bed behind the Purple Hills, she had counted her babies as they tucked their heads under their wings.

Little Joe Otter had been fishing and he brought a great fat brother of the lamented Tommy Trout, who didn't mind.

Jerry Muskrat brought up from the mud of the river bottom some fine fresh water clams, of which he is very fond.

Jimmy Skunk stole three big eggs from the nest of old Gray Goose.

Peter Rabbit and Jumper the Hare rolled up a great, tender, fresh cabbage.

Boomer the Nighthawk said that he was very sorry, but he was on a diet of insects, which he must swallow one at a time, so to save trouble he had swallowed them as he caught them.

Now Hooty the Owl is a glutton and is lazy. "Reddy Fox and Jimmy Skunk and Billy Mink are sure to bring something I like, so what is the use of spending my time hunting for what someone else will get for me?" said he to himself. So Hooty the Owl went very early to the Lone

Pine and hid among the thick branches where no one could see him.

Shadow the Weasel is sly and a thief and lives by his wits. So because he had rather steal than be honest, he too went to the midnight spread with nothing but his appetite.

Now Reddy Fox is also a glutton and very, very crafty. When he saw the plump duck brought by Billy Mink, his mouth watered, for Reddy Fox is very, very fond of young spring ducks. So straightway he began to plan how he could get possession of Billy Mink's duck.

And when Billy Mink saw the fat trout Little Joe Otter had brought, his eyes danced and his heart swelled with envy, for Billy Mink is very, very fond of fish. At once he began to plan how he could secure that particular fat trout Little Joe Otter guarded so carefully.

Jimmy Skunk was quite contented with the eggs he had stolen from old Gray Goose—that is, he was until he saw the plump chicken Reddy Fox had brought from Farmer Brown's dooryard.

Then suddenly his stomach became very empty, very empty indeed for chicken, and Jimmy Skunk began to think of a way to add the chicken of Reddy Fox to his own stolen eggs.

Because Reddy Fox is the largest he was given the place of honor at the head of the table under the Lone Pine. On his right sat Little Joe Otter and on his left Jerry Muskrat. Shadow the Weasel was next to Little Joe Otter, while right across from him was Jimmy Skunk. Peter Rabbit was next, sitting opposite his cousin, Jumper the Hare. At the extreme end, facing Reddy Fox, sat Billy Mink, with the plump duck right under his sharp little nose.

Boomer the Nighthawk excused himself on the plea that he needed exercise to aid digestion, and as he had brought nothing to the feast, his excuse was politely accepted.

Reddy Fox is very, very cunning, and his crafty brain had been busily working out a plan to get all these good things for himself. "Little brothers of the Green Meadows," began Reddy Fox, "we have met here to-night for a feast of brotherly love."

Reddy Fox paused a moment to look hungrily at Billy Mink's duck. Billy Mink cast a longing eye at Little Joe Otter's trout, while Jimmy Skunk stole an envious glance at Reddy Fox's chicken.

"But there is one missing to make our joy complete," continued Reddy Fox. "Who has seen Bobby Coon?"

No one had seen Bobby Coon. Somehow happy-go-lucky Bobby Coon had been overlooked when the invitations were sent out.

"I move," continued Reddy Fox, "that because Billy Mink runs swiftly, and because he knows where Bobby Coon usually is to be found, he be appointed a committee of one to find Bobby Coon and bring him to the feast."

Now nothing could have been less to the liking of Billy Mink, but there was nothing for him to do but to yield as gracefully as he could and go in search of Bobby Coon.

No sooner had Billy Mink disappeared down the Lone Little Path than Reddy Fox recalled a nest of grouse eggs he had seen that day under a big hemlock, and he proposed that inasmuch as Jimmy Skunk already wore stripes for having stolen a nest of eggs from Mrs. Grouse, he was just the one to go steal these eggs and bring them to the feast.

Of course there was nothing for Jimmy Skunk to do but to yield as gracefully as he could and go in search of the nest of eggs under the big hemlock.

No sooner had Jimmy Skunk started off than Reddy Fox remembered a big shining sucker Farmer Brown's boy had caught that afternoon and tossed among the rushes beside the Smiling Pool. Little Joe Otter listened and his mouth watered and watered until he could sit still no longer. "If you please," said Little Joe Otter, "I'll run down to the Smiling Pool and get that sucker to add to the feast."

No sooner was Little Joe Otter out of sight than Reddy Fox was reminded of a field of carrots on the other side of the Green Meadows. Now Peter Rabbit and Jumper the Hare are very fond of tender young carrots and they volunteered to bring a supply for the feast. So away they hurried with big jumps down the Lone Little Path and out across the Green Meadows.

No sooner were Peter Rabbit and Jumper the Hare fairly started than Reddy Fox began to tell of some luscious sweet apples he had noticed under a wild apple tree a little way back on the hill. Now Jerry Muskrat is quite as fond of luscious sweet apples as of freshwater clams, so quietly slipping away, he set out in quest of the wild apple tree a little way back on the hill.

No sooner was Jerry Muskrat lost in the black shadows than Reddy Fox turned to speak to Shadow the Weasel. But Shadow the Weasel believes that a feast in the stomach is worth two banquets untasted, so while the others had been talking, he had quietly sucked dry the three big eggs stolen by Jimmy Skunk from old Gray Goose, and then because he is so slim and so quick and so sly, he slipped away without anyone seeing him.

So when Reddy Fox turned to speak to Shadow the Weasel, he found himself alone. At least he thought himself alone, and he smiled a wicked, selfish smile as he walked over to Billy Mink's duck. He was thinking how smart he had been to get rid of all the others, and of how he would enjoy the feast all by himself.

As Reddy Fox stooped to pick up Billy Mink's duck, a great shadow dropped softly, oh so softly, out of the Lone Pine down onto the plump chicken. Then without the teeniest, weeniest bit of noise, it floated back into the Lone Pine and with it went the plump chicken.

Reddy Fox, still with his wicked, selfish smile, trotted back with Billy Mink's duck, but he dropped it in sheer surprise when he discovered that his plump chicken had disappeared. Now Reddy Fox is very suspicious, as people who are not honest themselves are very apt to be. So he left Billy Mink's duck where he had dropped it and trotted very, very softly up the Lone Little Path to try to catch the thief who had stolen his plump chicken.

No sooner was his back turned than down out of the Lone Pine floated the great shadow, and when a minute later Reddy Fox returned, Billy Mink's duck had also disappeared.

Reddy Fox could hardly believe his eyes. He didn't smile now. He was too angry and too frightened. Yes, Reddy Fox was frightened. He walked in a big circle round and round the place where the plump chicken and the duck had been, and the more he walked, the more suspicious he became. He wrinkled and wrinkled his little black nose in an effort to smell the intruder, but not a whiff could he get. All was as still and peaceful as could be. Little Joe Otter's trout lay shining in the moonlight. The big head of cabbage lay just where Peter Rabbit and Jumper the Hare had left it. Reddy Fox rubbed his eyes to make sure that he was not dreaming and that the plump chicken and the duck were not there too.

Just then Bowser the Hound, over at Farmer Brown's, bayed at the moon. Reddy Fox always is nervous and by this time he was so fidgety that he couldn't stand still. When Bowser the Hound bayed at the moon Reddy Fox jumped a foot off the ground and whirled about in the direction of Farmer Brown's house. Then he remembered that Bowser the Hound is always chained up at night, so that he had nothing to fear from him.

After listening and looking a moment Reddy Fox decided that all was safe. "Well," said he to himself, "I'll have that fat trout anyway," and turned to get it.

But the fat trout he had seen a minute before shining in the moonlight had also disappeared. Reddy Fox looked and looked until his eyes nearly popped out of his head. Then he did what all cowards do—ran home as fast as his legs could carry him.

Now of course Billy Mink didn't find Bobby Coon, and when he came back up the Lone Little Path he was very tired, very hungry and very cross. And of course Jimmy Skunk failed to find the nest of Mrs. Grouse, and Little Joe Otter could find no trace of the shining big sucker among the rushes beside the Smiling Pool. They also were very tired, very hungry and very cross.

When the three returned to the Lone Pine and found nothing there but the big head of cabbage, which none of them liked, the empty egg shells of old Gray Goose and Jerry Muskrat's clams, they straightway fell to accusing each other of having stolen the duck and the fat trout and the eggs and began to quarrel dreadfully.

Pretty soon up came Peter Rabbit and Jumper the Hare, who had failed to find the tender young carrots. And up came Jerry Muskrat, who had found no luscious sweet apples.

"Where is Reddy Fox?" asked Peter Rabbit.

Sure enough, where was Reddy Fox? Billy Mink and Little Joe Otter and Jimmy Skunk stopped quarreling and looked at each other.

"Reddy Fox is the thief!" they cried all together.

Peter Rabbit and Jumper the Hare and Jerry Muskrat agreed that Reddy Fox must be the thief, and had sent them all away on false errands that he might have the feast all to himself.

So because there was nothing else to do, Billy Mink and Little Joe Otter, tired and hungry and angry, started for their homes beside the Laughing Brook. And Jimmy Skunk, also tired and hungry and angry, started off up the Crooked Little Path to look for some beetles.

But Peter Rabbit and Jumper the Hare sat down to enjoy the big head of cabbage, while close beside them sat Jerry Muskrat smacking his lips over his clams, they tasted so good. Mother Moon looked down and smiled and smiled, for she knew that each had a clear conscience, for they had done no harm to anyone.

And up in the thick top of the great pine Hooty the Owl nodded sleepily, for his stomach was very full of chicken and duck and trout, although he had not been invited to the party.

And this is why Reddy Fox has no true friends on the Green Meadows.

CHAPTER III

~

WHY PETER RABBIT'S EARS ARE LONG

The Merry Little Breezes of Old Mother West Wind were tired. Ever since she had turned them out of her big bag onto the Green Meadows early that morning they had romped and played tag and chased butterflies while Old Mother West Wind herself went to hunt for a raincloud which had wandered away before it had watered the thirsty little plants who were bravely trying to keep the Green Meadows lovely and truly green. Jolly, round, red Mr. Sun wore his broadest smile and the more he smiled the warmer it grew. Mr. Sun is never thirsty himself, never the least little bit, or perhaps he would have helped Old Mother West Wind find the wandering raincloud.

The Merry Little Breezes threw themselves down on the edge of the Smiling Pool, where the rushes grow tall, and there they took turns rocking the cradle which held Mrs. Redwing's four babies.

Pretty soon one of the Merry Little Breezes, peeping through the rushes, spied Peter Rabbit sitting up very straight on the edge of the Green Meadows. His long ears were pointed straight up, his big eyes were very wide open and he seemed to be looking and listening with a great deal of curiosity.

"I wonder why it is that Peter Rabbit has such long ears," said the Merry Little Breeze.

"Chug-a-rum!" replied a great, deep voice right behind him.

All the Merry Little Breezes jumped up and ran through the rushes to the very edge of the Smiling Pool. There on a great green lily pad sat Great-Grandfather Frog, his hands folded across his white and yellow waistcoat and his green coat shining spick and span.

"Chug-a-rum," said Grandfather Frog.

"Oh, Grandfather Frog," cried the Merry Little Breezes all together, "do tell us why it is that Peter Rabbit has such long ears."

Grandfather Frog cleared his throat. He looked to the east and cleared his throat again. Then he looked to the west, and cleared his throat. He looked north and he looked south, and each time he cleared his throat, but said nothing. Finally he folded his hands once more over his white and yellow waistcoat, and looking straight up at jolly, round, red Mr. Sun he remarked in his very deepest voice and to no one in particular:

"If I had four fat, foolish, green flies, it is just possible that I might remember how it happens that Peter Rabbit has such long ears."

Then up jumped all the Merry Little Breezes and away they raced. Some of them went east, some of them went west, some of them went north, some of them went south, all looking for fat, foolish, green flies for Grandfather Frog.

By and by they came skipping back, one by one, to the edge of the Smiling Pool, each with a fat, foolish, green fly, and each stopping to give Mrs. Redwing's cradle a gentle push.

When Grandfather Frog had swallowed all the fat, foolish, green flies brought by the Merry Little Breezes, he settled himself comfortably on his big lily pad once more and began:

"Once upon a time, very long ago, when the world was young, Mr. Rabbit—not our Peter Rabbit, but his grandfather a thousand times removed—had short ears like all the other meadow people, and also his four legs were all of the same length, just exactly the same length.

"Now Mr. Rabbit had a great deal of curiosity, a very great deal, indeed. He was forever pushing his prying little nose into other people's affairs, which, you know, is a most unpleasant habit. In fact, Mr. Rabbit had become a nuisance.

"Whenever Billy Mink stopped to pass the time of day with Jerry Muskrat they were sure

Mr. Rabbit had a great deal of curiosity,
a very great deal, indeed. *Page 164.*

to find Mr. Rabbit standing close by, listening to all they said. If Johnny Chuck's mother ran over to have a few minutes' chat with Jimmy Skunk's mother, the first thing they knew Mr. Rabbit would be squatting down in the grass right behind them.

"The older he grew the worse Mr. Rabbit became. He would spend his evenings going from house to house, tiptoeing softly up to the windows to listen to what the folks inside were saying. And the more he heard the more Mr. Rabbit's curiosity grew.

"Now, like most people who meddle in other folks' affairs, Mr. Rabbit had no time to tend to his own business. His cabbage patch grew up to weeds. His house leaked, his fences fell to pieces, and altogether his was the worst looking place on the Green Meadows.

"Worse still, Mr. Rabbit was a trouble maker. He just couldn't keep his tongue still. And like most gossips, he never could tell the exact truth.

"Dear me! dear me!" said Grandfather Frog, shaking his head solemnly. "Things had come to a dreadful pass on the Green Meadows. Reddy Fox and Bobby Coon never met without fighting. Jimmy Skunk and Johnny Chuck turned their backs on each other. Jerry Muskrat, Little Joe Otter, and Billy Mink called each other bad names. All because Mr. Rabbit had told so many stories that were not true.

"Now when old Mother Nature visited the Green Meadows she soon saw what a dreadful state all the meadow people were in, and she began to inquire how it all came about.

"'It's all because of Mr. Rabbit,' said Reddy Fox.

"'No one is to blame but Mr. Rabbit,' said Striped Chipmunk.

"Everywhere old Mother Nature inquired it was the same—Mr. Rabbit, Mr. Rabbit, Mr. Rabbit.

"So then old Mother Nature sent for blustering great Mr. North Wind, who is very strong. And she sent for Mr. Rabbit.

"Mr. Rabbit trembled in his shoes when he got old Mother Nature's message. He would have liked to run away and hide. But he did not dare do that, for he knew that there was nowhere he could hide that Mother Nature would not find him sooner or later. And besides, his curiosity would give him no peace. He just *had* to know what old Mother Nature wanted.

"So Peter Rabbit put on his best suit, which was very shabby, and set out for the Lone Pine to see what old Mother Nature wanted. When he got there, he found all the little people of the Green Meadows and all the little folks of the Green Forest there before him. There were Reddy Fox, Johnny Chuck, Striped Chipmunk, Happy Jack Squirrel, Mr. Black Snake, old Mr. Crow, Sammy Jay, Billy Mink, Little Joe Otter, Jerry Muskrat, Spotty the Turtle, old King Bear, his cousin, Mr. Coon, and all the other little people.

"When he saw all who had gathered under the Lone Pine, and how they all looked crossly at him, Mr. Rabbit was so frightened that his heart went pit-a-pat, pit-a-pat, pit-a-pat, and he wanted more than ever to run away. But he didn't dare to. No, Sir, he didn't dare to. And then

Mr. Rabbit was so frightened that his
heart went pit-a-pat. *Page 168.*

he was so curious to know what it all meant that he wouldn't have run if he had dared.

"Old Mother Nature made Mr. Rabbit sit up on an old log where all could see him. Then in turn she asked each present who was the cause of all the trouble on the Green Meadows. And each in turn answered 'Mr. Rabbit.'

"'Mr. Rabbit,' said old Mother Nature, 'you are lazy, for your cabbage patch has all gone to weeds. You are shiftless, for your house leaks. You are a sneak, for you creep up where you are not wanted and listen to things which do not concern you. You are a thief, for you steal the secrets of others. You are a prevaricator, for you tell things which are not so. Mr. Rabbit, you are all these—a lazy, shiftless sneak, thief and prevaricator.'

"It was dreadful. Mother Nature paused, and Mr. Rabbit felt oh so ashamed. He did not look up, but he felt, he just *felt,* all the eyes of all the little meadow people and forest folk burning right into him. So he hung his head and two great tears fell splash, right at his feet. You see

Mr. Rabbit wasn't altogether bad. It was just this dreadful curiosity.

"Old Mother Nature knew this and down in her heart she loved Mr. Rabbit and was oh so sorry for him.

"'Mr. Rabbit,' continued old Mother Nature, 'because your curiosity is so great, your ears shall be made long, that every one who sees you may know that it is not safe to talk when you are near. Because you are a sneak and steal up to people unseen, your hind legs shall be made long, so that whenever you sit up straight you will be tall and every one can see you, and whenever you run, you will go with great jumps, and every one will know who it is running away. And because you are shiftless and your house leaks, you will hereafter live in a hole in the ground.'

"Then old Mother Nature took Mr. Rabbit by his two ears and big, strong Mr. North Wind took Peter Rabbit by his hind legs, and they both pulled. And when they put him down Peter Rabbit's ears and his hind legs were long, many times longer than they used to be. When he tried to run away to hide his shame, he found that the only way he could go was with great jumps, and you may be sure he jumped as fast as he could.

"And ever since that long ago time, when the world was young, rabbits have had long ears and long hind legs, all because of the curiosity of their grandfather a thousand times removed. And now you know why Peter Rabbit's ears are long, and why he is always sitting up and listening," concluded Great-Grandfather Frog.

"Thank you, thank you, Grandfather Frog!" shouted all the Merry Little Breezes, and raced away to help old Mother West Wind drive up the wandering raincloud, which she had found at last.

CHAPTER IV

~

REDDY FOX DISOBEYS

On the brow of the hill by the Lone Pine sat Reddy Fox. Every few moments he pointed his little black nose up at the round, yellow moon and barked. Way over across the broad White Meadows, which in summer time are green, you know, in the dooryard of Farmer Brown's house, Bowser the Hound sat and barked at the moon, too.

"Yap-yap-yap," barked Reddy Fox, as loud as he could.

"Bow-wow-wow," said Bowser the Hound in his deepest voice.

Then both would listen and watch the million little stars twinkle and twinkle in the frosty sky.

Now just why Reddy Fox should bark at the moon he did not know. He just had to. Every night for a week he had sat at the foot of the Lone Pine and barked and barked until his throat was sore. Every night old Mother Fox had warned him that noisy children would come to no good end, and every night Reddy had promised that he would bark no more. But every night when the first silver flood of witching light crept over the hill and cast strange shadows from the naked branches of the trees, Reddy forgot all about his promise. Deep down under his little red coat was a strange feeling which he could not explain. He simply *must* bark, so up to the Lone Pine he would go and yap and yap and yap, until all the little meadow people who were not asleep knew just where Reddy Fox was.

Bowser the Hound knew, too, and he made up his mind that Reddy Fox was making fun of him. Now Bowser did not like to be made fun of any more than little boys and girls do, and he made up his mind that if ever he could break his chain, or that if ever Farmer Brown forgot to chain him up, he would teach Reddy Fox a lesson that Reddy would never forget.

"Yap-yap-yap," barked Reddy Fox, and then listened to hear Bowser's deep voice reply. But this time there was no reply. Reddy listened, and listened, and then tried it again. Way off on a distant hill he could hear Hooty the Owl. Close by him Jack Frost was busy snapping sticks. Down on the White Meadows he could see Jimmy Skunk prowling about. Once he heard a rooster crow sleepily in Farmer Brown's hen-house, but he thought of Bowser the Hound, and though his mouth watered, he did not dare risk a closer acquaintance with the big dog. So he sat still and barked, and pretty soon he forgot all else but the moon and the sound of his own voice.

Now Bowser the Hound had managed to slip his collar. "Aha," thought Bowser, "now I'll teach Reddy Fox to make fun of me," and like a shadow he slipped through the fence and across the White Meadows towards the Lone Pine.

Reddy Fox had just barked for the hundreth time when he heard a twig crack just back of him.

It had a different sound from the noisy crack of Jack Frost, and Reddy stopped a yap right in the middle and whirled about to see what it might be. There was Bowser the Hound almost upon him, his eyes flashing fire, his great, red jaws wide open, and every hair on his back bristling with rage.

Reddy Fox didn't wait to say "Good evening," or to see more. Oh, no! He turned a back somersault and away he sped over the hard, snowy crust as fast as his legs could carry him. Bowser baying at the moon he liked to hear, but Bowser baying at his heels was another matter, and Reddy ran as he had never run before. Down across the White Meadows he sped, Bowser frightening all the echoes with the roar of his big voice as he followed in full cry.

How Reddy did wish that he had minded Mother Fox! How safe and snug and warm was his home under the roots of the old hickory tree, and how he did wish that he was safely there! But it would never do to go there now, for that would tell Bowser where he lived, and Bowser would take Farmer Brown there, and that would be the end of Reddy Fox and of Mother Fox and of all the brother and sister foxes.

So Reddy twisted and turned, and ran this way and ran that way, and the longer he ran, the shorter his breath grew. It was coming in great pants now. His bushy tail, of which he was so proud, had become very heavy. How Reddy Fox did wish and wish that he had minded Mother Fox! He twisted and turned, and doubled this way and that way, and all the time Bowser the Hound got closer and closer.

Now way off on the hill behind the White Meadows Mother Fox had been hunting for her supper. She had heard the "Yap-yap-yap" of Reddy Fox as he barked at the moon, and she had heard Bowser baying over in the barnyard of Farmer Brown. Then she had heard the "yap" of Reddy Fox cut short in the middle and the roar of Bowser's big voice as he started to chase Reddy Fox. She knew that Reddy could run fast, but she also knew that Bowser the Hound had a wonderful nose, and that Bowser would never give up.

So Mother Fox pattered down the Crooked Little Path onto the White Meadows, where she could see the chase. When she got near enough, she barked twice to tell Reddy that she would help him.

Now Reddy Fox was so tired that he was almost in despair when he heard Mother Fox bark. But he knew that Mother Fox was so wise, and she had so often fooled Bowser the Hound, that if he could hold out just a little longer she would help him. So for a few minutes he ran faster than ever and he gained a long way on Bowser the Hound. As he passed a shock of corn that had been left standing on the White Meadows, Mother Fox stepped out from behind it. "Go home, Reddy Fox," said she, sharply, "go home and stay there until I come." Then she deliberately sat down in front of the shock of corn to wait until Bowser the Hound should come in sight.

Now Bowser the Hound kept his eyes and nose on the track of Reddy Fox, looking up only once in a while to see where he was going, so he did not see Reddy Fox slip behind the corn shock, and when he did look up, he saw only Mother Fox sitting there waiting for him.

Now Bowser the Hound thinks slowly. When he saw old Mother Fox sitting there, he did not stop to think that it was not Reddy Fox whom he had been following, or he would have known better than to waste his time following old Mother Fox. He would have just hunted around until he had found where Reddy had gone to. But Bowser the Hound thinks slowly. When he saw old Mother Fox sitting there, he thought it was Reddy Fox and that now he had him.

With a great roar of his big voice, he sprang forward. Mother Fox waited until he was almost upon her, then springing to one side, she trotted off a little way. At once Bowser the Hound started after her. She pretended to be very tired. Every time he rushed forward she managed to just slip out of his grasp.

Little by little she led him across the White Meadows back towards Farmer Brown's barnyard. Pretty soon old Mother Fox began to run as fast as she could, and that is very fast indeed. She left Bowser the Hound a long, long way behind. When she came to a stone wall she jumped up on the stone wall and ran along it, just like a squirrel. Every once in a while she would make a long jump and then trot along a little way again. She knew that stones do not carry the scent well, and that Bowser the Hound would have hard work to smell her on the stone wall. Way down at the end of the pasture an old apple tree stretched a long limb out towards the stone wall. When she got opposite to this she jumped onto this long limb and ran up into the tree. There in the crotch, close to the trunk, she sat and watched.

Bowser the Hound, making a tremendous noise, followed her trail up to the stone wall. Then he was puzzled. He sniffed this way, and he sniffed that way, but he could not tell where Mother Fox had disappeared to. He looked up at old Mother Moon and bayed and bayed, but old Mother Moon did not help him a bit. Then he jumped over the stone wall and looked, and looked, and smelled, and smelled, but no track of

There in the crotch, close to the trunk,
she sat and watched. *Page 180.*

Mother Fox could he find. Then he ran up along the stone wall a little way, and then down along the stone wall a little way, but still he could not find a track of Mother Fox. The longer he hunted, the angrier he grew.

Old Mother Fox, sitting in the apple tree, watched him and laughed and laughed to herself. Then when she grew tired of watching him, she made a long jump out into the field and trotted off home to punish Reddy Fox for his disobedience. When she got there she found Reddy Fox very much ashamed, very tired and very sorrowful, and since that time Reddy Fox has never barked at the moon.

CHAPTER V

~

STRIPED CHIPMUNK'S POCKETS

I t was one of Striped Chipmunk's busy days.
Every day is a busy day with Striped Chipmunk
at this season of the year, for the sweet acorns
are ripe and the hickory nuts rattle down whenever Old Mother West Wind shakes the trees,
while every night Jack Frost opens chestnut burrs
just to see the squirrels scamper for the plump
brown nuts the next morning.

So Striped Chipmunk was very busy, very busy
indeed! He whisked in and out of the old stone
wall along one edge of the Green Meadows.
Back and forth, back and forth, sometimes to
the old hickory tree, sometimes to the hollow
chestnut tree, sometimes to the great oak on

the edge of the Green Forest Striped Chipmunk scampered.

Old Mother West Wind, coming down from the Purple Hills very early in the morning, had found Striped Chipmunk up before her and hard at work. Later, when jolly, round, red Mr. Sun had climbed up into the sky, the Merry Little Breezes had spied Striped Chipmunk whisking along the old stone wall and had raced over to play with him, for the Merry Little Breezes are very fond of Striped Chipmunk. They got there just in time to see him disappear under a great stone in the old wall. In a minute he was out again and off as fast as he could go to the old hickory tree.

"Oh, Striped Chipmunk, come play with us," shouted the Merry Little Breezes, running after him.

But Striped Chipmunk just flirted his funny little tail and winked with both his bright eyes at them.

"Busy! busy! busy!" said Striped Chipmunk, hurrying along as fast as his short legs could take him.

The Merry Little Breezes laughed, and one of them, dancing ahead, pulled the funny little tail of Striped Chipmunk.

"It's a beautiful day; do come and play with us," cried the Merry Little Breeze.

But Striped Chipmunk flirted his tail over his back once more.

"Busy! busy! busy!" he shouted over his shoulder and ran faster than ever.

In a few minutes he was back again, but such a queer-looking fellow as he was! His head was twice as big as it had been before and you would hardly have known that it was Striped Chipmunk but for the saucy way he twitched his funny little tail and the spry way he scampered along the old stone wall.

"Oh, Striped Chipmunk's got the mumps!" shouted the Merry Little Breezes.

But Striped Chipmunk said never a word. He couldn't. He ran faster than ever until he disappeared under the big stone. When he popped his head out again he was just his usual saucy little self.

"Say, Striped Chipmunk," cried the Merry Little Breezes, rushing over to him, "tell us how you happen to have pockets in your cheeks."

But Striped Chipmunk just snapped his bright eyes at them and said "Busy! busy! busy!" as he scuttled over to the hollow chestnut tree.

The Merry Little Breezes saw that it was no use at all to try to tempt Striped Chipmunk to play with them or to answer questions.

"I tell you what," cried one, "let's go ask Great-Grandfather Frog how Striped Chipmunk happens to have pockets in his cheeks. He'll know."

So away they started, after they had raced over to the big hollow chestnut tree and sent a shower of brown nuts rattling down to Striped Chipmunk from the burrs that Jack Frost had opened the night before.

"Good-bye, Striped Chipmunk," they shouted as they romped across the Green Meadows. And Striped Chipmunk stopped long enough to shout "Goodbye" before he filled his pockets with the brown nuts.

Old Grandfather Frog sat on his big green lily pad blinking in the sun. It was very still, very, very still indeed. Suddenly out of the brown bulrushes burst the Merry Little Breezes and surrounded old Grandfather Frog. And every one of them had brought to him a fat, foolish, green fly.

Grandfather's big goggly eyes sparkled and he gave a funny little hop up into the air as he caught each foolish green fly. When the last one was safely inside his white and yellow waistcoat he settled himself comfortably on the big green lily pad and folded his hands over the foolish green flies.

"Chug-a-rum!" said Grandfather Frog. "What is it you want this morning?"

"Oh, Grandfather Frog," cried the Merry Little Breezes, "tell us how it happens that Striped Chipmunk has pockets in his cheeks. Do tell us, Grandfather Frog. Please do!"

"Chug-a-rum," said Grandfather Frog. "How should I know?"

"But you do know, Grandfather Frog, you know you do. Please tell us!" cried the Merry Little Breezes as they settled themselves among the rushes.

And presently Grandfather Frog began:

"Once upon a time—a long, long while ago—"

"When the world was young?" asked a mischievous little Breeze.

Grandfather Frog pretended to be very much put out by the interruption, and tried to look very severe. But the Merry Little Breezes were all giggling, so that presently he had to smile too.

"Yes," said he, "it was when the world was young, before old King Bear became king. Mr. Chipmunk, Striped Chipmunk's great-great-great-grandfather a thousand times removed, was the smallest of the squirrels, just as Striped Chipmunk is now. But he didn't mind that, not the least little bit. Mr. Gray Squirrel was four times as big and had a handsome tail, Mr. Fox Squirrel was four times as big and he also had a handsome tail, Mr. Red Squirrel was twice as big and he thought his tail was very good to see. But Mr. Chipmunk didn't envy his big cousins their fine tails; not he! You see he had himself a beautiful striped coat of which he was very proud and which he thought much more to be desired than a big tail.

"So Mr. Chipmunk went his way happy and contented and he was such a merry little fellow and so full of fun and cut such funny capers that everybody loved Mr. Chipmunk.

"One day, when the nights were cool and all the trees had put on their brilliant colors, old Mother Nature sent word down across the Green Meadows that every squirrel should gather for her and store away until she came a thousand nuts. Now the squirrels had grown fat and lazy through the long summer, all but Mr. Chipmunk, who frisked about so much that he had no chance to grow fat.

"Mr. Gray Squirrel grumbled. Mr. Fox Squirrel grumbled. Mr. Red Squirrel grumbled. But they didn't dare disobey old Mother Nature, so they all set out, each to gather a thousand nuts. And Mr. Chipmunk alone was pleasant and cheerful.

"When they reached the nut trees, what do you suppose they discovered? Why, that they had been so greedy that they had eaten most of the nuts and it was going to be hard work to find and store a thousand nuts for old Mother Nature. Then they began to hurry, did Mr. Gray Squirrel and Mr. Fox Squirrel and Mr. Red Squirrel, each trying to make sure of his thousand nuts. They quarreled and they fought over the nuts on the ground and even up in the trees. And because they were so big and so strong, they pushed Mr. Chipmunk this way and they pushed him that way and often just as he was going to pick up a fat nut one of them would knock him over and make off with the prize.

"Poor Mr. Chipmunk kept his temper and was as polite as ever, but how he did work! His cousins are great climbers and could get the nuts still left on the trees, but Mr. Chipmunk is a poor climber, so he had to be content with those on the ground. Of course he could carry only one nut at a time and his legs were so short that he had to run as fast as ever he could to store each nut in his secret store-house and get back for another. And while the others quarreled and fought, he hurried back and forth, back and forth, from early morning until jolly, round, red Mr. Sun pulled his night cap on behind the Purple Hills, hunting for nuts and putting them away in his secret store-house.

"But the nuts grew scarcer and scarcer on the ground and harder to find, for the other squirrels were picking them up too, and then they did not have so far to carry them.

"Sometimes one of his cousins up in the trees would drop a nut, but Mr. Chipmunk never would take it, not even when he was having hard work to find any, 'for,' said he to himself, 'if my cousin drops a nut, it is his nut just the same.'

"Finally Mr. Gray Squirrel announced that he had got his thousand nuts. Then Mr. Fox Squirrel announced that he had got his thousand nuts. The next day Mr. Red Squirrel stopped hunting because he had his thousand nuts.

"But Mr. Chipmunk had hardly more than half as many. And that night he made a dreadful discovery—some one had found his secret store-house and had *stolen* some of his precious nuts.

"'It's of no use to cry over what can't be helped,' said Mr. Chipmunk, and the next morning he bravely started out again. He had worked so hard that he had grown thinner and thinner until now he was only a shadow of his old self. But he was as cheerful as ever and kept right on hunting and hunting for stray nuts. Mr. Gray Squirrel and Mr. Fox Squirrel and Mr. Red Squirrel sat around and rested and made fun of him. Way up in the tops of the tallest trees a few nuts still clung, but his cousins did not once offer to go up and shake them down for Mr. Chipmunk.

"And then old Mother Nature came down across the Green Meadows. First Mr. Gray Squirrel took her to his storehouse and she counted his thousand nuts. Then Mr. Fox Squirrel led her to his storehouse and she counted his thousand nuts. Then Mr. Red Squirrel showed her his store-house and she counted his thousand nuts.

"Last of all Mr. Chipmunk led her to his secret store-house and showed her the pile of nuts he had worked so hard to get. Old Mother Nature didn't need to count them to see that there were not a thousand there.

"'I've done the best I could,' said Mr. Chipmunk bravely, and he trembled all over, he was so tired.

"Old Mother Nature said never a word but went out on the Green Meadows and sent the Merry Little Breezes to call together all the little meadow people and all the little forest folks. When they had all gathered before her she suddenly turned to Mr. Gray Squirrel.

"'Go bring me a hundred nuts from your store-house,' said she.

"Then she turned to Mr. Fox Squirrel.

"'Go bring me a hundred nuts from your store-house,' said she.

"Last of all she called Mr. Red Squirrel out where all could see him. Mr. Red Squirrel crept out very slowly. His teeth chattered and his tail, of which he was so proud, dragged on the ground, for you see Mr. Red Squirrel had something on his mind.

"Then old Mother Nature told how she had ordered each squirrel to get and store for her a thousand nuts. She told just how selfish Mr. Gray Squirrel and Mr. Fox Squirrel had been. She told just how hard Mr. Chipmunk had worked and then she told how part of his precious store had been stolen.

"'And there,' said old Mother Nature in a loud voice so that every one should hear, 'there is the thief!'

"Then she commanded Mr. Red Squirrel to go to his store-house and bring her half of the biggest and best nuts he had there!

"Mr. Red Squirrel sneaked off with his head hanging, and began to bring the nuts. And as he tramped back and forth, back and forth, all the little meadow people and all the little forest folks pointed their fingers at him and cried 'Thief! Thief! Thief!'

"When all the nuts had been brought to her by Mr. Gray Squirrel and Mr. Fox Squirrel and Mr. Red Squirrel, old Mother Nature gathered them all up and put them in the secret store-house of Mr. Chipmunk. Then she set Mr. Chipmunk up on an old stump where all could see him and she said:

"'Mr. Chipmunk, because you have been faithful, because you have been cheerful, because you have done your best, henceforth you shall have two pockets, one in each cheek, so that you can carry two nuts at once, that you may not have to work so hard the next time I tell you to store a thousand nuts.'

"And all the little meadow people and all the little forest folks shouted 'Hurrah for Mr. Chipmunk!' All but his cousins, Mr. Gray Squirrel and Mr. Fox Squirrel and Mr. Red Squirrel, who hid themselves for shame.

"And ever since that time long ago, when the world was young, the Chipmunks have had pockets in their cheeks.

"You can't fool old Mother Nature," concluded Great-Grandfather Frog. "No, Sir, you can't fool old Mother Nature and it's no use to try."

"Thank you, thank you," cried the Merry Little Breezes, clapping their hands. Then they all raced across the Green Meadows to shake down some more nuts for Striped Chipmunk.

CHAPTER VI

~

REDDY FOX, THE BOASTER

J ohnny Chuck waddled down the Lone Little Path across the Green Meadows. Johnny Chuck was very fat and rolly-poly. His yellow brown coat fitted him so snugly that it seemed as if it must burst. Johnny Chuck was feeling very happy—very happy indeed, for you see Johnny Chuck long ago found the best thing in the world, which is contentment.

Jolly, round, red Mr. Sun, looking down from the sky, smiled and smiled to see Johnny Chuck waddling down the Lone Little Path, for he loved the merry-hearted little fellow, as do all the little meadow people—all but Reddy Fox, for Reddy Fox has not forgotten the surprise Johnny Chuck once gave him and how he called him a "'fraid cat."

Once in a while Johnny Chuck stopped to brush his coat carefully, for he is very particular about his appearance, is Johnny Chuck. By and by he came to the old butternut tree down by the Smiling Pool. He could see it a long time before he reached it, and up in the top of it he could see Blacky the Crow flapping his wings and cawing at the top of his voice.

"There must be something going on," said Johnny Chuck to himself, and began to waddle faster. He looked so very queer when he tried to hurry that jolly, round, red Mr. Sun smiled more than ever.

When he was almost to the old butternut tree Johnny Chuck sat up very straight so that his head came just above the tall meadow grasses beside the Lone Little Path. He could see the Merry Little Breezes dancing and racing under the old butternut tree and having such a good time! And he could see the long ears of Peter Rabbit standing up straight above the tall meadow grasses. One of the Merry Little Breezes spied Johnny Chuck.

"Hurry up, Johnny Chuck!" he shouted, and Johnny Chuck hurried.

When he reached the old butternut tree he was all out of breath. He was puffing and blowing and he was so warm that he wished just for a minute, a single little minute, that he could swim like Billy Mink and Jerry Muskrat and Little Joe Otter, so that he could jump into the Smiling Pool and cool off.

"Hello, Johnny Chuck!" shouted Peter Rabbit.

"Hello yourself, and see how you like it!" replied Johnny Chuck.

"Hello myself!" said Peter Rabbit.

And then because it was so very foolish everybody laughed. It is a good thing to feel foolishly happy on a beautiful sunshiny day, especially down on the Green Meadows.

Jimmy Skunk was there. He was feeling very, very good indeed, was Jimmy Skunk, for he had found some very fine beetles for his breakfast.

Little Joe Otter was there, and Billy Mink and Jerry Muskrat and Happy Jack Squirrel, and of course Reddy Fox was there. Oh my, yes, of course Reddy Fox was there! Reddy Fox never misses a chance to show off. He was wearing his very newest red coat and his whitest waistcoat. He had brushed his tail till it looked very handsome, and every few minutes he would turn and admire it. Reddy Fox thought himself a very fine gentleman. He admired himself and he wanted every one else to admire him.

"Let's do stunts," said Peter Rabbit. "I can jump farther than anybody here!"

Then Peter Rabbit jumped a tremendously long jump. Then everybody jumped, everybody but Reddy Fox. Even Johnny Chuck jumped, and because he was so rolly-poly he tumbled over and over and everybody laughed and Johnny Chuck laughed loudest of all.

And because his hind legs are long and meant for jumping Peter Rabbit had jumped farther than any one else.

"I can climb to the top of the old butternut tree quicker than anybody else," cried Happy Jack Squirrel, and away he started with Bobby Coon and Billy Mink after him, for though Billy Mink is a famous swimmer and can run swiftly, he can also climb when he has to. But Happy Jack Squirrel was at the top of the old butternut tree almost before the others had started.

The Merry Little Breezes clapped their hands and everybody shouted for Happy Jack Squirrel, everybody but Reddy Fox.

"I can swim faster than anybody here," shouted Little Joe Otter.

In a flash three little brown coats splashed into the Smiling Pool so suddenly that they almost upset Great-Grandfather Frog watching from his big green lily pad. They belonged to Little Joe Otter, Billy Mink and Jerry Muskrat. Across the Smiling Pool and back again they raced and Little Joe Otter was first out on the bank.

"Hurrah for Little Joe Otter!" shouted Blacky the Crow.

And everybody shouted "Hurrah!" Everybody but Reddy Fox.

"What can you do, Jimmy Skunk?" asked Peter Rabbit, dancing up and down, he was so excited.

Jimmy Skunk yawned lazily.

"I can throw a wonderful perfume farther than anybody here," said Jimmy Skunk.

"We know it! We know it!" shouted the Merry Little Breezes as everybody tumbled heels over head away from Jimmy Skunk, even Reddy Fox. "But please don't!"

And Jimmy Skunk didn't.

Then they all came back, Reddy Fox carefully brushing his handsome red coat which had become sadly mussed, he had fled in such a hurry.

Now for the first time in his life Johnny Chuck began to feel just a wee, wee bit discontented. What was there he could do better than any one else? He couldn't jump and he couldn't climb and he couldn't swim. He couldn't even run fast, because he was so fat and round and rolly-poly.

He quite forgot that he was so sunny-hearted and good-natured that everybody loved him, everybody but Reddy Fox.

Just then Reddy Fox began to boast, for Reddy Fox is a great boaster. "Pooh!" said Reddy Fox, "pooh! Anybody could jump if their legs were made for jumping. And what's the good of climbing trees anyway? Now *I* can run faster than anybody here—faster than anybody in the whole world!" said Reddy Fox, puffing himself out.

"Chug-a-rum," said Grandfather Frog. "You can't beat Spotty the Turtle."

Then everyone shouted and rolled over and over in the grass, they were so tickled, for every one remembered how Spotty the Turtle had once won a race from Reddy Fox.

For a minute Reddy Fox looked very foolish. Then he lost his temper, which is a very unwise thing to do, for it is hard to find again. He swelled himself out until every hair stood on end and he looked twice as big as he did before. He strutted up and down and glared at each in turn.

"And I'm not afraid of any living thing on the Green Meadows!" boasted Reddy Fox.

"Chug-a-rum," said Grandfather Frog. "Do I see Bowser the Hound?"

Every hair on Reddy Fox suddenly fell back into place. He whirled about nervously and anxiously looked over the Green Meadows. Then everybody shouted again and rolled over and over in the grass and held on to their sides, for you see Bowser the Hound wasn't there at all.

But everybody took good care to keep away from Reddy Fox, everybody but Johnny Chuck. He just sat still and chuckled and chuckled till his fat sides shook.

"What are you laughing at?" demanded Reddy Fox.

"I was just thinking," said Johnny Chuck, "that though you can run so fast, you can't even catch me."

Reddy Fox just glared at him for a minute, he was so mad. Then he sprang straight at Johnny Chuck.

"I'll show you!" he snarled.

"What are you laughing at?"
demanded Reddy Fox. *Page 204.*

Now Johnny Chuck had been sitting close beside a hole that Grandfather Chuck had dug a long time before and which was empty. In a flash Johnny Chuck disappeared head first in the hole. Now the hole was too small for Reddy Fox to enter, but he was so angry that he straightway began to dig it larger. My, how the sand did fly! It poured out behind Reddy Fox in a stream of shining yellow.

Johnny Chuck ran down the long tunnel underground until he reached the end. Then when he heard Reddy Fox digging and knew that he was really coming, Johnny Chuck began to dig, too, only instead of digging down he dug up towards the sunshine and the blue sky.

My, how his short legs did fly and his stout little claws dug into the soft earth! His little forepaws flew so fast that if you had been there you could hardly have seen them at all. And with his strong hind legs he kicked the sand right back into the face of Reddy Fox.

All the little meadow people gathered around the hole where Johnny Chuck and Reddy Fox had disappeared. They were very anxious, very anxious indeed. Would Reddy Fox catch Johnny Chuck? And what would he do to him? Was all their fun to end in something terrible to sunny-hearted, merry Johnny Chuck, whom everybody loved?

All of a sudden, pop! right out of the solid earth among the daisies and buttercups, just like a jack-in-the-box, came Johnny Chuck! He looked very warm and a little tired, but he was still chuckling as he scampered across to another hole of Grandfather Chuck's.

By and by something else crawled out of the hole Johnny Chuck had made. Could it be Reddy Fox? Where were his white waistcoat and beautiful red coat? And was that thing dragging behind him his splendid tail?

He crept out of the hole and then just lay down and panted for breath. He was almost too tired to move. Then he began to spit sand out of his mouth and blow it out of his nose and try to wipe it out of his eyes. The long hair of his fine coat was filled full of sand and no one

Then everybody shouted "Haw! haw! haw!" *Page 209.*

would ever have guessed that this was Reddy Fox.

"Haw! haw! haw!" shouted Blacky the Crow.

Then everybody shouted "Haw! haw! haw!" and began to roll in the grass and hold on to their sides once more; everybody but Reddy Fox. When he could get his breath he didn't look this way or that way, but just sneaked off to his home under the big hickory.

And when Old Mother West Wind came with her big bag to take the Merry Little Breezes to their home behind the Purple Hills, Johnny Chuck waddled back up the Lone Little Path chuckling to himself, for that little feeling of discontent was all gone. He had found that after all he could do something better than anybody else on the Green Meadows, for in his heart he knew that none could dig so fast as he.

CHAPTER VII

~

JOHNNY CHUCK'S SECRET

J ohnny Chuck pushed up the last bit of gravel from the hole he had dug between the roots of the old apple tree in a corner of the Green Meadows. He smoothed it down on the big, yellow mound he had made in front of his door. Then he sat up very straight on top of the mound, brushed his coat, shook the sand from his trousers and carefully cleaned his hands.

After he had rested a bit, he turned around and looked at his new home, for that is what it was, although he had not come there to live yet, and no one knew of it, no one but jolly, round, red Mr. Sun, who, peeping between the branches of the old apple tree, had caught Johnny Chuck at work. But *he* wouldn't tell, not jolly Mr. Sun! Looking down from the blue sky every day he sees all sorts of queer things and he learns all kinds of secrets, does Mr. Sun, but he never, never tells. No, Sir! Mr. Sun never tells one of them, not even to Old Mother West Wind when at night they go down together behind the Purple Hills.

So jolly, round, red Mr. Sun just smiled and smiled when he discovered Johnny Chuck's secret, for that is just what the new home under the apple tree was—a secret. Not even the Merry Little Breezes, who find out almost everything, had discovered it.

Johnny Chuck chuckled to himself as he planned a back door, a beautiful back door, hidden behind a tall clump of meadow grass where no one would think to look for a door. When he had satisfied himself as to just where he would put it, he once more sat up very straight on his nice, new mound and looked this way and looked that way to be sure that no one was near. Then he started for his old home along a secret little path he had made for himself.

Pretty soon he came to the Lone Little Path that went past his own home. He danced and he skipped along the Lone Little Path, and, because he was so happy, he tried to turn a somersault. But Johnny Chuck was so round and fat and rolly-poly that he just tumbled over in a heap.

"Well, well, well! What's the matter with you?" said a voice close beside him before he could pick himself up. It was Jimmy Skunk, who was out looking for some beetles for his dinner.

Johnny Chuck scrambled to his feet and looked foolish, very foolish indeed.

"There's nothing the matter with me, Jimmy Skunk," said Johnny. "There's nothing the matter with me. It's just because I've got a secret."

"A secret!" cried Jimmy Skunk. "What is it?"

"Yes, a secret, a really, truly secret," said Johnny Chuck, and looked very important.

"Tell me, Johnny Chuck. Come on, tell just *me,* and then we'll have the secret together," begged Jimmy Skunk.

Now Johnny Chuck was so tickled with his secret that it seemed as if he *must* share it with some one. He just couldn't keep it to himself any longer.

"You won't tell any one?" said Johnny Chuck.

Jimmy Skunk promised that he wouldn't tell a soul.

"Cross your heart," commanded Johnny Chuck.

Jimmy Skunk crossed his heart.

Then Johnny Chuck looked this way and looked that way to be sure that no one was listening. Finally he whispered in Jimmy Skunk's ear:

"I've got a new home under the old apple tree in a corner of the Green Meadows," said Johnny Chuck.

Of course Jimmy Skunk was very much surprised and very much interested, so Johnny Chuck told him all about it.

"Now, remember, it's a secret," said Johnny Chuck, as Jimmy Skunk started off down the Lone Little Path across the Green Meadows, to look for some beetles.

"I'll remember," said Jimmy Skunk.

"And don't tell!" called Johnny Chuck.

Jimmy Skunk promised that he wouldn't tell. Then Johnny Chuck started off up the Lone Little Path, whistling, and Jimmy Skunk trotted down the Lone Little Path onto the Green Meadows.

Jimmy Skunk was thinking so much about Johnny Chuck's new home that he quite forgot to look for beetles, and he almost ran into Peter Rabbit.

"Hello, Jimmy Skunk," said Peter Rabbit, "can't you see where you are going? It must be you have something on your mind; what is it?"

"I was thinking of Johnny Chuck's new home," said Jimmy Skunk.

"Johnny Chuck's new home!" exclaimed Peter Rabbit. "Has Johnny Chuck got a new home? Where is it?"

"Under the roots of the old apple tree in a corner of the Green Meadows," said Jimmy Skunk, and then he clapped both hands over his mouth. You see he hadn't really meant to tell. It just slipped out.

"Oh, but it's a secret!" cried Jimmy Skunk. "It's a secret, and you mustn't tell. I guess Johnny

Chuck won't mind if you know, Peter Rabbit, but you mustn't tell any one else." Peter Rabbit promised he wouldn't.

Now Peter Rabbit is very inquisitive, very inquisitive indeed. So as soon as he had parted from Jimmy Skunk he made up his mind that he must see the new home of Johnny Chuck. So off he started as fast as he could go towards the old apple tree in a corner of the Green Meadows. Half way there he met Reddy Fox.

"Hello, Peter Rabbit! Where are you going in such a hurry?" asked Reddy Fox.

"Over to the old apple tree to see Johnny Chuck's new home," replied Peter Rabbit as he tried to dodge past Reddy Fox. Then of a sudden he remembered and clapped both hands over his mouth.

"Oh, but it's a secret, Reddy Fox. It's a secret, and you mustn't tell!" cried Peter Rabbit.

But Reddy Fox wouldn't promise that he wouldn't tell, for in spite of his handsome coat and fine manners, Reddy Fox is a scamp. And, besides, he has no love for Johnny Chuck, for he has not forgotten how Johnny Chuck once made him run and called him a "'fraid cat."

So when Reddy Fox left Peter Rabbit he grinned a wicked grin and hurried off to find Bobby Coon. He met him on his way to the Laughing Brook. Reddy Fox told Bobby Coon all about Johnny Chuck's secret and then hurried away after Peter Rabbit, for Reddy Fox also is very inquisitive.

Bobby Coon went on down to the Laughing Brook. There he met Billy Mink and told him about the new home Johnny Chuck had made under the old apple tree in a corner of the Green Meadows.

Pretty soon Billy Mink met Little Joe Otter and told him.

Then Little Joe Otter met Jerry Muskrat and told him.

Jerry Muskrat saw Blacky the Crow and told him, and Great-Grandfather Frog heard him.

Blacky the Crow met his first cousin, Sammy Jay, and told him.

Sammy Jay met Happy Jack Squirrel and told him.

Happy Jack met his cousin, Striped Chipmunk, and told him.

Striped Chipmunk passed the house of old Mr. Toad and told him.

The next morning, very early, before Old Mother West Wind had come down from the Purple Hills, Johnny Chuck stole over to his new home to begin work on his new back door. He had hardly begun to dig when he heard some one cough right behind him. He whirled around and there sat Peter Rabbit looking as innocent and surprised as if he had really just discovered the new home for the first time.

"What a splendid new home you have, Johnny Chuck!" said Peter Rabbit.

"Y—e—s," said Johnny Chuck, slowly. "It's a secret," he added suddenly. "You won't tell, will you, Peter Rabbit?"

Peter Rabbit promised that he wouldn't tell. Then Johnny Chuck felt better and went back to work as soon as Peter Rabbit left.

He had hardly begun, however, when some one just above him said: "Good morning, Johnny Chuck."

Johnny Chuck looked up and there in the old apple tree sat Blacky the Crow and his cousin, Sammy Jay.

Just then there was a rustle in the grass and out popped Billy Mink and Little Joe Otter and Jerry Muskrat and Happy Jack Squirrel and Striped Chipmunk and Bobby Coon. When Johnny Chuck had recovered from his surprise and looked over to the doorway of his new home there sat Reddy Fox on Johnny Chuck's precious new mound. It seemed as if all the little meadow people were there, all but Jimmy Skunk, who wisely stayed away.

"We've come to see your new home," said Striped Chipmunk, "and we think it's the nicest home we've seen for a long time."

"It's so nicely hidden away, it's really quite secret," said Reddy Fox, grinning wickedly.

Just then up raced the Merry Little Breezes and one of them had a message for Johnny

Chuck from Great-Grandfather Frog. It was this:

"Whisper a secret to a friend and you shout it in the ear of the whole world."

After every one had admired the new home, they said good-bye and scattered over the Green Meadows. Then Johnny Chuck began to dig again, but this time he wasn't making his new back door. No indeed! Johnny Chuck was digging at that new mound of yellow gravel of which he had been so proud. Jolly, round, red Mr. Sun blinked to be sure that he saw aright, for Johnny Chuck was *filling up his new home* between the roots of the old apple tree. When he got through, there wasn't any new home.

Then Johnny Chuck brushed his coat carefully, shook the sand out of his trousers, wiped his hands and started off for his old home. And this time he didn't take his special hidden path, for Johnny Chuck didn't care who saw him go.

Late that afternoon, Johnny Chuck sat on his old doorstep, with his chin in his hands, watching Old Mother West Wind gathering her Merry

Little Breezes into the big bag in which she carries them to their home behind the Purple Hills.

"'Whisper a secret to a friend and you shout it in the ear of the whole world.' Now what did Grandfather Frog mean by that?" thought Johnny Chuck. "Now I didn't tell anybody but Jimmy Skunk and Jimmy Skunk didn't tell anyone but Peter Rabbit and—and—"

Then Johnny Chuck began to chuckle and finally to laugh. "'Whisper a secret to a friend and you shout it in the ear of the whole world.' My gracious, what a loud voice I must have had and didn't know it!" said Johnny Chuck, wiping the tears of laughter from his eyes.

And the next day Johnny Chuck started to make a new home. Where? Oh, that's Johnny Chuck's secret. And no one but jolly, round, red Mr. Sun has found it out yet.

CHAPTER VIII

~

JOHNNY CHUCK'S GREAT FIGHT

Johnny Chuck sat on the doorstep of his new home, looking away across the Green Meadows. Johnny Chuck felt very well satisfied with himself and with all the world. He yawned lazily and stretched and stretched and then settled himself comfortably to watch the Merry Little Breezes playing down by the Smiling Pool.

By and by he saw Peter Rabbit go bobbing along down the Lone Little Path. Lipperty, lipperty, lip, went Peter Rabbit and every other jump he looked behind him.

"Now what is Peter Rabbit up to?" said Johnny Chuck to himself, "and what does he keep looking behind him for?"

Johnny Chuck sat up a little straighter to watch Peter Rabbit hop down the Lone Little Path. Then of a sudden he caught sight of something that made him sit up straighter than ever and open his eyes very wide. Something was following Peter Rabbit. Yes, Sir, something was bobbing along right at Peter Rabbit's heels.

Johnny Chuck forgot the Merry Little Breezes. He forgot how warm it was and how lazy he felt. He forgot everything else in his curiosity to learn what it could be following so closely at Peter Rabbit's heels.

Presently Peter Rabbit stopped and sat up very straight and then—Johnny Chuck nearly tumbled over in sheer surprise! He rubbed his eyes to make sure that he saw aright, for there were *two* Peter Rabbits! Yes, Sir, there were two Peter Rabbits, only one was very small, very small indeed.

"Oh!" said Johnny Chuck, "that must be Peter Rabbit's baby brother!"

Then he began to chuckle till his fat sides shook. There sat Peter Rabbit with his funny long ears standing straight up, and there right behind him, dressed exactly like him, sat Peter Rabbit's baby brother with *his* funny little long ears standing straight up. When Peter Rabbit wiggled his right ear, his baby brother wiggled *his* right ear. When Peter Rabbit scratched his left ear, his baby brother scratched *his* left ear. Whatever Peter Rabbit did, his baby brother did too.

Presently Peter Rabbit started on down the Lone Little Path—lipperty, lipperty, lip, and right at his heels went his baby brother—lipperty, lipperty, lip. Johnny Chuck watched them out of sight, and then he settled himself on his doorstep once more to enjoy a sun bath. Every once in a while he chuckled to himself as he remembered how funny Peter Rabbit's baby brother had looked. Presently Johnny Chuck fell asleep.

Jolly, round, red Mr. Sun had climbed quite high in the sky when Johnny Chuck awoke. He yawned and stretched and stretched and yawned, and then he sat up to look over the Green Meadows. Then he became wide awake, very wide awake indeed! Way down on the Green Meadows he caught a glimpse of something red jumping about in the long meadow grass.

"That must be Reddy Fox," thought Johnny Chuck. "Yes, it surely is Reddy Fox. Now I wonder what mischief he is up to."

Then he saw all the Merry Little Breezes racing towards Reddy Fox as fast as they could go. And there was Sammy Jay screaming at the top of his voice, and his cousin, Blacky the Crow. Happy Jack Squirrel was dancing up and down excitedly on the branch of an old elm close by.

Johnny Chuck waited to see no more, but started down the Lone Little Path to find out what it all was about. Half way down the Lone Little Path he met Peter Rabbit running as hard as he could. His long ears were laid flat back, his big eyes seemed to pop right out of his head, and he was running as Johnny Chuck had never seen him run before.

"What are you running so for, Peter Rabbit?" asked Johnny Chuck.

"To get Bowser the Hound," shouted Peter Rabbit over his shoulder, as he tried to run faster.

"Now what can be the matter?" said Johnny Chuck to himself, "to send Peter Rabbit after Bowser the Hound?" He knew that, like all the other little meadow people, there was nothing of which Peter Rabbit was so afraid as Farmer Brown's great dog, Bowser the Hound.

Johnny Chuck hurried down the Lone Little Path as fast as his short legs could take his fat, rolly-poly self.

Presently he came out onto the Green Meadows, and there he saw a sight that set every nerve in his round little body a-tingle with rage.

Reddy Fox had found Peter Rabbit's baby brother and was doing his best to frighten him to death.

"I'm going to eat you now," shouted Reddy Fox, and then he sprang on Peter Rabbit's baby brother and gave him a cuff that sent him heels over head sprawling in the grass.

"Coward! Coward, Reddy Fox!" shrieked Sammy Jay.

"Shame! Shame!" shouted the Merry Little Breezes.

"You're nothing but a great big bully!" yelled Blacky the Crow.

But no one did anything to help Peter Rabbit's baby brother, for Reddy Fox is so much bigger than any of the rest of them, except Bobby Coon, that all the little meadow people are afraid of him.

But Reddy Fox just laughed at them, and nipped the long ears of Peter Rabbit's little brother so hard that he cried with the pain.

Now all were so intent watching Reddy Fox torment the baby brother of Peter Rabbit that no one had seen Johnny Chuck coming down the Lone Little Path. And for a few minutes no one recognized the furious little yellow-brown bundle that suddenly knocked Reddy Fox over and seized him by the throat. You see it didn't look a bit like Johnny Chuck. Every hair was standing on end, he was so mad, and this made him appear twice as big as they had ever seen him before.

"Coward! Coward! Coward!" shrieked Johnny Chuck as he shook Reddy Fox by the throat. And then began the greatest fight that the Green Meadows had ever seen.

Now Johnny Chuck is not naturally a fighter. Oh my, no! He is so good-natured and so sunny-hearted that he seldom quarrels with any one. But when he has to fight, there isn't a cowardly hair on him, not the teeniest, weeniest one. No one ever has a chance to cry, "'Fraid cat! Cry baby!" after Johnny Chuck.

So though, like all the other little meadow people, he was usually just a little afraid of Reddy Fox, because Reddy is so much bigger, he forgot all about it as soon as he caught sight of Reddy Fox tormenting Peter Rabbit's little brother. He didn't stop to think of what might happen to himself. He didn't stop to think at all. He just gritted his teeth and in a flash had Reddy Fox on his back.

Such a fight was never seen before on the Green Meadows! Reddy Fox is a bully and a coward, for he never fights with any one of his own size if he can help it, but when he has to fight, he fights hard. And he certainly had to fight now.

"Bully!" hissed Johnny Chuck as with his stout little hind feet he ripped the bright red coat of Reddy Fox. "You great big bully!"

Over and over they rolled, Johnny Chuck on top, then Reddy Fox on top, then Johnny Chuck up again, clawing and snarling.

It seemed as if news of the fight had gone over all the Green Meadows, for the little meadow people came running from every direction—Billy Mink, Little Joe Otter, Jerry Muskrat, Striped Chipmunk, Jimmy Skunk, old Mr. Toad. Even Great-Grandfather Frog, who left his big lily pad, and came hurrying with great jumps across the Green Meadows. They formed a ring around Reddy Fox and Johnny Chuck and danced with excitement. And all wanted Johnny Chuck to win.

Peter Rabbit's poor little brother, so sore and lame from the knocking about from Reddy Fox, and so frightened that he hardly dared breathe, lay flat on the ground under a little bush and was forgotten by all but the Merry Little Breezes, who covered him up with some dead grass, and kissed him and whispered to him not to be afraid now. How Peter Rabbit's little brother did hope that Johnny Chuck would win! His great, big, round, soft eyes were wide with terror as he thought of what might happen to him if Reddy Fox should whip Johnny Chuck.

But Reddy Fox wasn't whipping Johnny Chuck. Try as he would, he could not get a good hold on that round, fat, little body. And Johnny Chuck's stout claws were ripping his red coat and white vest and Johnny Chuck's sharp teeth were gripping him so that they could not be shaken loose. Pretty soon Reddy Fox began to think of nothing but getting away. Every one was shouting for Johnny Chuck. Every time Reddy Fox was underneath, he would hear a great shout from all the little meadow people, and he knew that they were glad.

Now Johnny Chuck was round and fat and rolly-poly, and when one is round and fat and rolly-poly, one's breath is apt to be short. So it was with Johnny Chuck. He had fought so hard that his breath was nearly gone. Finally he loosed his hold on Reddy Fox for just a second to draw in a good breath. Reddy Fox saw his chance, and, with a quick pull and spring, he broke away.

How all the little meadow people did scatter! You see they were very brave, very brave indeed, so long as Johnny Chuck had Reddy Fox down, but now that Reddy Fox was free, each one was suddenly afraid and thought only of himself. Jimmy Skunk knocked Jerry Muskrat flat in his hurry to get away. Billy Mink trod on Great-Grandfather Frog's big feet and didn't even say "Excuse me." Striped Chipmunk ran head first into a big thistle and squealed as much from fear as pain.

But Reddy Fox paid no attention to any of them. He just wanted to get away, and off he started, limping as fast as he could go up the Lone Little Path. Such a looking sight! His beautiful red coat was in tatters. His face was scratched. He hobbled as he ran. And just as he broke away, Johnny Chuck made a grab and pulled a great mouthful of hair out of the splendid tail Reddy Fox was so proud of.

When the little meadow people saw that Reddy Fox was actually running away, they stopped running themselves, and all began to shout: "Reddy Fox is a coward and a bully! Coward! Coward!" Then they crowded around Johnny Chuck and all began talking at once about his great fight.

Just then they heard a great noise up on the hill. They saw Reddy Fox coming back down the Lone Little Path, and he was using his legs just as well as he knew how. Right behind him, his great mouth open and waking all the echoes with his big voice, was Bowser the Hound.

You see, although Peter Rabbit couldn't fight for his little baby brother and is usually very, very timid, he isn't altogether a coward. Indeed, he had been very brave, very brave indeed. He had gone up to Farmer Brown's and had jumped right under the nose of Bowser the Hound. Now that is something that Bowser the Hound never can stand. So off he had started after Peter Rabbit. And Peter Rabbit had started back for the Green Meadows as fast as his long legs could take him, for he knew that if once Bowser the Hound caught sight of Reddy Fox, he would forget all about such a little thing as a saucy rabbit.

Sure enough, half way down the Lone Little Path they met Reddy Fox sneaking off home, and, when Bowser the Hound saw him, he straightway forgot all about Peter Rabbit, and, with a great roar, started after Reddy Fox.

When Johnny Chuck had carefully brushed his coat and all the little meadow people had wished him good luck, he started off up the Lone Little Path for home, the Merry Little Breezes dancing ahead and Peter Rabbit coming lipperty, lipperty, lip behind, and right between them hopped Peter Rabbit's little brother, who thought Johnny Chuck the greatest hero in the world.

When they reached Johnny Chuck's old home, Peter Rabbit and Peter Rabbit's little brother tried to tell him how thankful they were to him, but Johnny Chuck just laughed and said: "It was nothing at all, just nothing at all."

When at last all had gone, even the Merry Little Breezes, Johnny Chuck slipped away to his new home, which is his secret, you know, which no one knows but jolly, round, red Mr. Sun, who won't tell.

"I hope," said Johnny Chuck, as he stretched himself out on the mound of warm sand by his doorway, for he was very tired, "I hope," said Johnny Chuck, sighing contentedly, "that Reddy Fox got away from Bowser the Hound!"

And Reddy Fox did.

～

CHAPTER IX

MR. TOAD'S OLD SUIT

Peter Rabbit was tired and very sleepy as he hopped along the Crooked Little Path down the hill. He could see Old Mother West Wind just emptying her Merry Little Breezes out of her big bag onto the Green Meadows to play all the bright summer day. Peter Rabbit yawned and yawned again as he watched them dance over to the Smiling Pool. Then he hopped on down the Crooked Little Path towards home.

Sammy Jay, sitting on a fence post, saw him coming.

"Peter Rabbit out all night!
Oh my goodness what a sight!

Peter Rabbit, reprobate!
No good end will be your fate!"

shouted Sammy Jay.

Peter Rabbit ran out his tongue at Sammy Jay.

"Who stole Happy Jack's nuts? Thief! Thief! Thief!" shouted Peter Rabbit at Sammy Jay, and kept on down the Crooked Little Path.

It was true—Peter Rabbit had been out all night playing in the moonlight, stealing a midnight feast in Farmer Brown's cabbage patch and getting into mischief with Bobby Coon. Now when most of the little meadow people were just waking up Peter Rabbit was thinking of bed.

Presently he came to a big piece of bark which is the roof of Mr. Toad's house. Mr. Toad was sitting in his doorway blinking at jolly, round, red Mr. Sun, who had just begun to climb up the sky.

"Good morning, Mr. Toad," said Peter Rabbit.

"Good morning," said Mr. Toad.

"You're looking very fine this morning, Mr. Toad," said Peter Rabbit.

"I'm feeling very fine this morning," said Mr. Toad.

"Why, my gracious, you have on a new suit, Mr. Toad!" exclaimed Peter Rabbit.

"Well, what if I have, Peter Rabbit?" demanded Mr. Toad.

"Oh, nothing, nothing, nothing at all, Mr. Toad, nothing at all," said Peter Rabbit hastily, "only I didn't know you ever had a new suit. What have you done with your old suit, Mr. Toad?"

"Swallowed it," said Mr. Toad shortly, turning his back on Peter Rabbit.

And that was all Peter Rabbit could get out of Mr. Toad, so he started on down the Crooked Little Path. Now Peter Rabbit has a great deal of curiosity and is forever poking into other people's affairs. The more he thought about it the more he wondered what Mr. Toad could have done with his old suit. Of course he hadn't *swallowed* it! Who ever heard of such a thing! The more he thought of it the more Peter Rabbit felt that he must know what Mr. Toad had done with his old suit. By this time he had forgotten that he had been out all night. He had forgotten that he was sleepy. He had got to find out about Mr. Toad's old suit.

"I'll just run over to the Smiling Pool and ask Grandfather Frog. He'll surely know what Mr. Toad does with his old suits," said Peter Rabbit, and began to hop faster.

When he reached the Smiling Pool there sat Great-Grandfather Frog on his big green lily pad as usual. There was a hungry look in his big goggly eyes, for it was so early that no foolish, green flies had come his way yet. But Peter Rabbit was too full of curiosity in Mr. Toad's affairs to notice this.

"Good morning, Grandfather Frog," said Peter Rabbit.

"Good morning," replied Grandfather Frog a wee bit gruffly.

"You're looking very fine this morning, Grandfather Frog," said Peter Rabbit.

"Not so fine as I'd feel if I had a few fat, foolish, green flies," said Grandfather Frog.

"I've just met your cousin, Mr. Toad, and he has on a new suit," said Peter Rabbit.

"Indeed!" replied Grandfather Frog. "Well, I think it's high time."

"What does Mr. Toad do with his old suit, Grandfather Frog?" asked Peter Rabbit.

"Chug-a-rum! It's none of my business. Maybe he swallows it," replied Grandfather Frog crossly, and turned his back on Peter Rabbit.

Peter Rabbit saw that his curiosity must remain unsatisfied. He suddenly remembered that he had been out all night and was very, very sleepy, so he started off home across the Green Meadows.

Now the Merry Little Breezes had heard all that Peter Rabbit and Grandfather Frog had said, and they made up their minds that they would find out from Grandfather Frog what Mr. Toad really did do with his old suit. First of all they scattered over the Green Meadows. Presently back they all came, each blowing ahead of him a fat, foolish, green fly. Right over to the big green lily pad they blew the green flies.

"Chug-a-rum! Chug-a-rum! Chug-a-rum!" said Grandfather Frog, as each fat, foolish, green fly disappeared inside his white and yellow waist-coat. When the last one was out of sight, all but a leg which was left sticking out of a corner of Grandfather Frog's big mouth, one of the Merry Little Breezes ventured to ask him what became of Mr. Toad's old suit.

Grandfather Frog settled himself comfortably on the big green lily pad and folded his hands across his white and yellow waistcoat.

"Chug-a-rum," began Grandfather Frog. "Once upon a time—"

The Merry Little Breezes clapped their hands and settled themselves among the buttercups and daisies, for they knew that soon they would know what Mr. Toad did with his old suit.

"Once upon a time," began Grandfather Frog again, "when the world was young, old King Bear received word that old Mother Nature would visit the Green Meadows and the Green Forest.

Of course old King Bear wanted his kingdom and his subjects to look their very best, so he issued a royal order that every one of the little meadow people and every one of the little forest folk should wear a new suit on the day that old Mother Nature was to pay her visit.

"Now like old King Bear, every one wanted to appear his very best before old Mother Nature, but as no one knew the exact day she was to come, every one began at once to wear his best suit, and to take the greatest care of it. Old King Bear appeared every day in a suit of glossy black. Lightfoot the Deer, threw away his dingy gray suit, and put on a coat of beautiful red and fawn. Mr. Mink, Mr. Otter, Mr. Muskrat, Mr. Rabbit, Mr. Woodchuck, Mr. Coon, who you know was first cousin to old King Bear, Mr. Gray Squirrel, Mr. Fox Squirrel, Mr. Red Squirrel, all put on brand new suits. Mr. Skunk changed his black and white stripes for a suit of all black, very handsome, very handsome indeed. Mr. Chipmunk took care to see that his new suit had the most beautiful stripes to be obtained.

"Mr. Jay, who was something of a dandy, had a wonderful new coat that looked for all the world as it if had been cut from the bluest patch of sky and trimmed with edging taken from the whitest clouds. Even Mr. Crow and Mr. Owl took pains to look their very best.

"But Mr. Toad couldn't see the need of such a fuss. He thought his neighbors spent altogether too much time and thought on dress. To be sure he was anxious to look his best when old Mother Nature came, so he got a new suit all ready. But Mr. Toad couldn't afford to sit around in idleness admiring his new clothes. No indeed! Mr. Toad had too much to do. He was altogether too busy. He had a large garden to take care of, had Mr. Toad, and work in a garden is very hard on clothes. So Mr. Toad just wore his old suit over his new one and went on about his business.

"By and by the great day came when old Mother Nature arrived to inspect the kingdom of old King Bear. All the little meadow people and all the little forest folk hastened to pay their respects to old Mother Nature and to strut about in their fine clothes—all but Mr. Toad. He was so busy that he didn't even know that old Mother Nature had arrived.

"Late in the afternoon, Mr. Toad stopped to rest. He had just cleared his cabbage patch of the slugs which threatened to eat up his crop and he was very tired. Presently he happened to look up the road, and who should he see but old Mother Nature herself coming to visit his garden and to find out why Mr. Toad had not been to pay her his respects.

"Suddenly Mr. Toad remembered that he had on his working clothes, which were very old, very dirty and very ragged. For just a minute he didn't know what to do. Then he dived under a cabbage leaf and began to pull off his old suit. But the old suit stuck! He was in such a hurry and so excited that he couldn't find the buttons. Finally he got his trousers off. Then he reached over and got hold of the back of his coat and tugged and hauled until finally he pulled his old coat off right over his head just as if it were a shirt.

"Mr. Toad gave a great sigh of relief as he stepped out in his new suit, for you remember that he had been wearing that new suit underneath the old one all the time.

"Mr. Toad was very well pleased with himself until he thought how terribly untidy that ragged old suit looked lying on the ground. What should he do with it? He couldn't hide it in the garden, for old Mother Nature's eyes are so sharp that she would be sure to see it. What should he do?

"Then Mr. Toad had a happy thought. Every one made fun of his big mouth. But what was a big mouth for if not to use? He would swallow his old suit! In a flash Mr. Toad dived under the cabbage leaf and crammed his old suit into his mouth.

"When old Mother Nature came into the garden, Mr. Toad was waiting in the path to receive her. Very fine he looked in his new suit and you would have thought he had been waiting all day to receive old Mother Nature, but for one thing— swallow as much and as hard as he would, he couldn't get down quite all of his old suit, and a leg of his trousers hung out of a corner of his big mouth.

"Of course old Mother Nature saw it right away. And how she did laugh! And of course Mr. Toad felt very much mortified. But Mother Nature was so pleased with Mr. Toad's garden and with Mr. Toad's industry that she quite overlooked the ragged trousers leg hanging from the corner of Mr. Toad's mouth.

"'Fine clothes are not to be compared with fine work,' said old Mother Nature. 'I herewith appoint you my chief gardener, Mr. Toad. And as a sign that all may know that this is so, hereafter you shall always swallow your old suit whenever you change your clothes!'

"And from that day to this the toads have been the very best of gardeners. And in memory of their great, great, great-grandfather a thousand times removed they have always swallowed their old suits.

"Now you know what my cousin, old Mr. Toad, did with his old suit just before Peter Rabbit passed his house this morning," concluded Great-Grandfather Frog.

"Oh," cried the Merry Little Breezes, "thank you, thank you, Grandfather Frog!"

Then they raced away across the Green Meadows and up the Crooked Little Path to see if old Mr. Toad was gardening. And Peter Rabbit still wonders what old Mr. Toad did with his old suit.

CHAPTER X

~

GRANDFATHER FROG GETS EVEN

Old Grandfather Frog sat on his big green lily pad in the Smiling Pool dreaming of the days when the world was young and the frogs ruled the world. His hands were folded across his white and yellow waistcoat. Round, red, smiling Mr. Sun sent down his warmest rays on the back of Grandfather Frog's green coat.

Very early that morning Old Mother West Wind, hurrying down from the Purple Hills on her way to help the white-sailed ships across the great ocean, had stopped long enough to blow three or four fat, foolish, green flies over to the big lily pad, and they were now safely inside the white and yellow waistcoat. A thousand little tadpoles, the great, great-grandchildren of Grandfather Frog, were playing in the Smiling Pool, and every once in a while wriggling up to the big lily pad to look with awe at Grandfather Frog and wonder if they would ever be as handsome and big and wise as he.

And still old Grandfather Frog sat dreaming and dreaming of the days when all the frogs had tails and ruled the world.

Presently Billy Mink came hopping and skipping down the Laughing Brook. Sometimes he swam a little way and sometimes he ran a little way along the bank, and sometimes he jumped from stone to stone. Billy Mink was feeling very good—very good indeed. He had caught a fine fat trout for breakfast. He had hidden two more away for dinner in a snug little hole no one knew of but himself. Now he had nothing to do but get into mischief. You can always depend upon Billy Mink to get into mischief. He just can't help it.

So Billy Mink came hopping and skipping down the Laughing Brook to the Smiling Pool. Then he stopped, as still as the rock he was standing on, and peeped through the bulrushes. Billy Mink is very cautious, very cautious indeed. He always looks well before he shows himself, that nothing may surprise him.

So Billy Mink looked all over the Smiling Pool and the grassy banks. He saw the sunbeams dancing on the water. He saw the tadpoles having such a good time in the Smiling Pool. He saw the Merry Little Breezes kissing the buttercups and daisies on the bank, and he saw old Grandfather Frog with his hands folded across his white and yellow waistcoat sitting on the green lily pad, dreaming of the days when the world was young.

Then Billy Mink took a long breath, a very long breath, and dived into the Smiling Pool. Now, Billy Mink can swim very fast, very fast indeed. For a little way he can swim even faster than Mr. Trout. And he can stay under water a long time.

Straight across the Smiling Pool, with not even the tip of his nose out of water, swam Billy Mink. The thousand little tadpoles saw him coming and fled in all directions to bury themselves in the mud at the bottom of the Smiling Pool, for when he thinks no one is looking Billy Mink sometimes gobbles up a fat tadpole for breakfast.

Straight across the Smiling Pool swam Billy Mink toward the big green lily pad where Grandfather Frog sat dreaming of the days when the world was young. When he was right under the big green lily pad he suddenly kicked up hard with his hind feet. Up went the big green lily pad, and, of course, up went Grandfather Frog—up and over flat on his back, with a great splash into the Smiling Pool!

Now, Grandfather Frog's mouth is very big. Indeed, no one else has so big a mouth, unless it be his cousin, old Mr. Toad. And when Grandfather Frog went over flat on his back, splash in the Smiling Pool, his mouth was wide open.

You see he was so surprised he forgot to close it. So, of course, Grandfather Frog swallowed a great deal of water, and he choked and spluttered and swam around in foolish little circles trying

He was so surprised he forgot to close it. *Page 252.*

to find himself. Finally he climbed out on his big green lily pad.

"Chug-a-rum!" said Grandfather Frog, and looked this way and looked that way. Then he gave a funny hop and turned about in the opposite direction and looked this way and looked that way, but all he saw was the Smiling Pool dimpling and smiling, Mrs. Redwing bringing a fat worm to her hungry little babies in their snug nest in the bulrushes, and the Merry Little Breezes hurrying over to see what the trouble might be.

"Chug-a-rum!" said Grandfather Frog. "It is very strange. I must have fallen asleep and had a bad dream."

Then he once more settled himself comfortably on the big green lily pad, folded his hands across his white and yellow waistcoat, and seemed to be dreaming again, only his big goggly eyes were not dreaming. No, indeed! They were very much awake, and they saw all that was going on in the Smiling Pool. Great-Grandfather Frog was just pretending. You may fool him once, but

Grandfather Frog has lived so long that he has become very wise, and though Billy Mink is very smart, it takes some one a great deal smarter than Billy Mink to fool Grandfather Frog twice in the same way.

Billy Mink, hiding behind the Big Rock, had laughed and laughed till he had to hold his sides when Grandfather Frog had choked and spluttered and hopped about on the big lily pad trying to find out what it all meant. He thought it such a good joke that he couldn't keep it to himself, so when he saw Little Joe Otter coming to try his slippery slide he swam across to tell him all about it. Little Joe Otter laughed and laughed until he had to hold *his* sides. Then they both swam back to hide behind the Big Rock to watch until Grandfather Frog should forget all about it, and they could play the trick over again.

Now, out of the corner of one of his big goggly eyes, Grandfather Frog had seen Billy Mink and Little Joe Otter with their heads close together, laughing and holding their sides, and he saw them swim over behind the Big Rock. Pretty soon one of the Merry Little Breezes danced over to see if Grandfather Frog had really gone to sleep. Grandfather Frog didn't move, not the teeniest, weeniest bit, but he whispered something to the Merry Little Breeze, and the Merry Little Breeze flew away, shaking with laughter, to where the other Merry Little Breezes were playing with the buttercups and daisies.

Then all the Merry Little Breezes clapped their hands and laughed too. They left the buttercups and daisies and began to play tag across the Smiling Pool.

Now, right on the edge of the Big Rock lay a big stick. Pretty soon the Merry Little Breezes danced over to the Big Rock, and then, suddenly, all together they gave the big stick a push. Off it went, and then such a splashing and squealing as there was behind the Big Rock!

In a few moments Little Joe Otter crept out beside his slippery slide and slipped away holding on to his head. And, sneaking through the bulrushes, so as not to be seen, crawled Billy Mink, back towards his home on the Laughing

Brook. Billy Mink wasn't laughing now. Oh, no! He was limping and he was holding on to his head. Little Joe Otter and Billy Mink had been sitting right underneath the big stick.

"Chug-a-rum!" said Grandfather Frog and held on to his sides and opened his mouth very wide in a noiseless laugh, for Grandfather Frog never makes a sound when he laughs.

"Chug-a-rum!" said Grandfather Frog once more. Then he folded his hands across his white and yellow waistcoat and began again to dream of the days when the frogs had long tails and ruled the world.

CHAPTER XI

～

THE DISAPPOINTED BUSH

Way down beside the Laughing Brook grew a little bush. It looked a whole lot like other little bushes all around it. But really it was quite different, as you shall see. When in the spring warm, jolly, round Mr. Sun brought back the birds and set them singing, when the little flowers popped their heads out of the ground to have a look around, then all the little bushes put out their green leaves.

This little bush of which I am telling you put out its green leaves with the rest. The little leaves grew bigger and bigger on all the little bushes. By and by on some of the other little bushes, little brown buds began to appear and grow and grow.

Then on more and more of the little bushes the little brown buds came and grew and grew. But on this little bush of which I am telling you no little brown buds appeared. The little bush felt very sad indeed.

Pretty soon all the little brown buds on the other little brown bushes burst their brown coats, and then all the little bushes were covered with little flowers. Some were white and some were yellow and some were pink; and the air was filled with the sweet odor of all the little flowers. It brought the bees from far, far away to gather the honey, and all the little bushes were very happy indeed.

But the little bush of which I am telling you had no little flowers, for you see it had had no little buds, and it felt lonely and shut away from the other little bushes, and very sad indeed. But it bravely kept on growing and growing and growing. Its little leaves grew bigger and bigger and bigger, and it tried its best not to mind because it had no little flowers.

Then one by one, and two by two, and three by three, and finally in whole showers, the little flowers of all the other little bushes fell off, and they looked very much like the little bush of which I am telling you, so that the little bush no longer felt sad.

All summer long all the little bushes grew and grew and grew. The birds came and built their nests among them. Peter Rabbit and his brothers and sisters scampered under them. The butterflies flew over them.

By and by came the fall, and with the fall came Jack Frost. He went about among the little bushes, pinching the leaves. Then the little green leaves turned to brown and red and yellow and pretty soon they fluttered down to the ground, the Merry Little Breezes blew them about and all the little bushes were bare. They had no leaves at all to cover their little naked brown limbs.

The little bush of which I am telling you lost its leaves with the rest. But all the summer long this little bush had been growing some of those little brown buds, which the other bushes had had in the spring, and now, when all the other little bushes had lost all the green leaves, and had nothing at all upon their little brown twigs, behold! one beautiful day, the little bush of which I am telling you was covered with gold, for each little brown bud had burst its little brown coat and there was a beautiful little yellow flower. Such a multitude of these little yellow flowers! They covered the little bush from top to bottom. Then the little bush felt very happy indeed, for it was the only bush which had any flowers. And every one who passed that way stopped to look at it and to praise it.

Colder grew the weather and colder. Johnny Chuck tucked himself away to sleep all winter. Grandfather Frog went deep, deep down in the mud, not to come out again until spring. By and by the little yellow flowers dropped off the little bush, just as the other little flowers in spring had dropped off the other bushes. But they left behind them tiny little packages, one for every little flower that had been on the bush. All winter long these little packages clung to the little bush. In the spring when the little leaves burst forth in all the little bushes, these little packages on the little bush of which I am telling you grew and grew and grew. While the other little bushes had a lot of little flowers as they had had the year before, these little brown packages on the little bush of which I am telling you kept on growing. And they comforted the little bush because it felt that it really had something worth while.

All the summer long the little brown packages grew and grew until they looked like little nuts. When the fall came again and all the little leaves dropped off all the little bushes, and the little bush of which I am telling you was covered with another lot of little yellow flowers and was very happy, then these little brown nuts, one bright autumn day, suddenly popped open! And out of each one flew two brown shiny little seeds. You never saw such a popping and a snapping and a jumping! Pop! pop! snap! snap! hippetty hop! they went, faster than the corn pops in the corn popper. Reddy Fox, who always is suspicious, thought some one was shooting at him. Down on the ground fell the little brown shining seeds and tucked themselves into the warm earth under the warm leaves, there to stay all winter long.

And when the third spring came with all its little birds and all its little flowers and the warm sunshine, every one of these little brown seeds which had tucked themselves into the warm earth, burst its little brown skin, and up into the sunshine came a little green plant, which would grow and grow and grow, and by and by become just like the little bush I am telling you about.

When the little bush looked down and saw all these little green children popping out of the ground, it was very happy indeed, for it knew that it would no longer be lonely. It no longer felt bad when all the other bushes were covered with flowers, for it knew that by and by when all the other little bushes had lost all their leaves and all their flowers, then would come its turn, and it knew that for a whole year its little brown children would be held safe on its branches.

Now, what do you think is the name of this little bush? Why, it is the witch hazel. And sometime when you fall down and bump yourself hard grandma will go to the medicine closet and will bring out a bottle, and from that bottle she will pour something on that little sore place and it will make it feel better. Do you know what it is? It is the gift of the witch hazel bush to little boys and big men to make them feel better when they are hurt.

CHAPTER XII

~

WHY BOBBY COON WASHES HIS FOOD

Happy-go-lucky Bobby Coon sat on the edge of the Laughing Brook just as round, red Mr. Sun popped up from behind the Purple Hills and Old Mother West Wind turned all her Merry Little Breezes out to romp on the Green Meadows.

Bobby Coon had been out all night. You see Bobby Coon is very apt to get into mischief, and because usually it is safer to get into mischief under cover of the darkness Bobby Coon prefers the night wherein to go abroad. Not that Bobby Coon is really bad! Oh my, no! Everybody likes Bobby Coon. But he can no more keep out of mischief than a duck can keep out of water.

So Bobby Coon sat on the edge of the Laughing Brook and he was very busy, very busy indeed. He was washing his breakfast. Really, it was his dinner, for turning night into day just turns everything topsy-turvy. So Bobby Coon eats dinner when most of the little meadow people are eating breakfast.

This morning he was very busy washing a luscious ear of sweet corn just in the milk. He dipped it in the water and with one little black paw rubbed it thoroughly. Then he looked it over carefully before, with a sigh of contentment, he sat down to put it in his empty little stomach. When he had finished it to the last sweet, juicy kernel, he ambled sleepily up the Lone Little Path to the big hollow chestnut tree where he lives, and in its great hollow in a soft bed of leaves Bobby Coon curled himself up in a tight little ball to sleep the long, bright day away.

One of the Merry Little Breezes softly followed him. When he had crawled into the hollow chestnut and only his funny, ringed tail hung out, the Merry Little Breezes tweaked it sharply just for fun, and then danced away down the Lone Little Path to join the other Merry Little Breezes around the Smiling Pool.

"Oh! Grandfather Frog," cried a Merry Little Breeze, "tell us why it is that Bobby Coon always washes his food. He never eats it where he gets it or takes it home to his hollow in the big chestnut, but always comes to the Laughing Brook to wash it. None of the other meadow people do that."

Now Great-Grandfather Frog is counted very wise. He is very, very old and he knows the history of all the tribes of little meadow people way back to the time when the frogs ruled the world.

When the Merry Little Breeze asked him why Bobby Coon always washes his food, Grandfather Frog stopped to snap up a particularly fat, foolish, green fly that came his way. Then, while all the Merry Little Breezes gathered around him, he settled himself on his big green lily pad and began:

"Once upon a time, when the world was young, old King Bear ruled in the Green Forest. Of course old Mother Nature, who was even more beautiful then than she is now, was the real ruler, but she let old King Bear think he ruled so long as he ruled wisely.

"All the little Green Forest folk and all the little people of the Green Meadows used to take presents of food to old King Bear, so that he never had to hunt for things to eat. He grew fatter and fatter and fatter until it seemed as if his skin must burst. And the fatter he grew the lazier he grew."

Grandfather Frog paused with an expectant far-away look in his great bulging eyes. Then he leaped into the air so far that when he came down it was with a great splash in the Smiling Pool. But as he swam back to his big lily pad the leg of a foolish green fly could be seen sticking out of one corner of his big mouth, and he settled himself with a sigh of great contentment.

"Old King Bear," continued Grandfather Frog, just as if there had been no interruption, "grew fatter and lazier every day, and like a great many other fat and lazy people who have nothing to do for themselves but are always waited on by others, he grew shorter and shorter in temper and harder and harder to please.

"Now perhaps you don't know it, but the Bear family and the Coon family are very closely related. In fact, they are second cousins. Old Mr. Coon, Bobby Coon's father with a thousand greats tacked on before, was young then, and he was very, very proud of being related to old King Bear. He began to pass some of his old playfellows on the Green Meadows without seeing them. He spent a great deal of time brushing his coat and combing his whiskers and caring for his big ringed tail. He held his head very high and he put on such airs that pretty soon he could see no one at all but members of his own family and of the royal family of Bear.

"Now as old King Bear grew fat and lazy he grew fussy, so that he was no longer content to take everything brought him, but picked out the choicest portions for himself and left the rest. Mr. Coon took charge of all the things brought as tribute to old King Bear and of course where there were so many goodies left he got all he wanted without working.

"So just as old King Bear had grown fat and lazy and selfish, Mr. Coon grew fat and lazy and selfish. Pretty soon he began to pick out the best things for himself and hide them before old King Bear saw them. When old King Bear was asleep he would go get them and stuff himself like a greedy pig. And because he was stealing and wanted no one to see him he always ate his stolen feasts at night.

"Now old Mother Nature is, as you all know, very, very wise, oh very wise indeed. One of the first laws she made when the world was young is that every living thing shall work for what it has, and the harder it works the stronger it shall grow. So when Old Mother Nature saw how fat and lazy and selfish old King Bear was getting and how fat and lazy and dishonest his cousin, Mr. Coon, was becoming, she determined that they should be taught a lesson which they would remember for ever and ever and ever.

"First she proclaimed that old King Bear should be king no longer, and no more need the little folks of the Green Forest and the little people of the Green Meadows bring him tribute.

"Now when old Mother Nature made this proclamation old King Bear was fast asleep. It was just on the edge of winter and he had picked out a nice warm cave with a great pile of leaves for a bed. Old Mother Nature peeped in at him. He was snoring and probably dreaming of more good things to eat. 'If he is to be king no longer, there is no use in waking him now,' said old Mother Nature to herself, 'he is so fat and so stupid. He shall sleep until gentle Sister South Wind comes in the spring to kiss away the snow and ice. Then he shall waken with a lean stomach and a great appetite and there shall be none to feed him.'

"Now old Mother Nature always has a warm heart and she was very fond of Bobby Coon's grandfather a thousand times removed. So when she saw what a selfish glutton and thief he had become she decided to put him to sleep just as she had old King Bear. But first she would teach Mr. Coon that stolen food is not the sweetest.

"So old Mother Nature found some tender, juicy corn just in the milk which Mr. Coon had stolen from old King Bear. Then she went down on the Green Meadows where the wild mustard grows and gathering a lot of this she rubbed the juice into the corn and then put it back where Mr. Coon had left it.

"Now I have told you that it was night when Mr. Coon had his stolen feasts, for he wanted no one to see him. So no one was there when he took a great bite of the tender, juicy corn old Mother Nature had put back for him. Being greedy and a glutton, he swallowed the first mouthful before he had fairly tasted it, and took a second, and then such a time as there was on the edge of the Green Forest! Mr. Coon rolled over and over with both of his forepaws clasped over his stomach and groaned and groaned and groaned. He had rubbed his eyes and of course had got mustard into them and could not see. He waked up all the little Green Forest folk who sleep through the night, as good people should, and they all gathered around to see what was the matter with Mr. Coon.

"Finally old Mother Nature came to his relief and brought him some water. Then she led him to his home in the great hollow in the big chestnut tree, and when she had seen him curled up in a tight little ball among the dried leaves she put him into the long sleep as she had old King Bear.

"In the spring, when gentle Sister South Wind kissed away all the snow and ice, old King Bear, who was king no longer, and Mr. Coon awoke and both were very thin, and both were very hungry, oh very, very hungry indeed. Old King Bear, who was king no longer, wasn't the least mite fussy about what he had to eat, but ate gladly any food he could find.

"But Mr. Coon remembered the burning of his stomach and mouth and could not forget it. So whenever he found anything to eat he first took it to the Laughing Brook or the Smiling Pool and washed it very carefully, lest there be some mustard on it.

"And ever since that long ago time, when the world was young, the Coon family has remembered that experience of Mr. Coon, who was second cousin to old King Bear, and that is why Bobby Coon washes his food, travels about at night, and sleeps all winter," concluded Grandfather Frog, fixing his great goggle eyes on a foolish green fly headed his way.

"Oh thank you, thank you, Grandfather Frog," cried the Merry Little Breezes as they danced away over the Green Meadows. But one of them slipped back long enough to get behind the foolish green fly and blow him right up to Grandfather Frog's big lily pad.

"Chug-a-rum," said Grandfather Frog, smacking his lips.

CHAPTER XIII

~

THE MERRY LITTLE BREEZES HAVE A BUSY DAY

Old Mother West Wind came down from the Purple Hills in the shadowy coolness of the early morning, before even jolly, round, red Mr. Sun had thrown off his rosy coverlids for his daily climb up through the blue sky. The last little star was blinking sleepily as Old Mother West Wind turned her big bag upside down on the Green Meadows and all her children, the Merry Little Breezes, tumbled out on the soft green grass.

Then Old Mother West Wind kissed them all around and hurried away to hunt for a rain cloud which had gone astray. The Merry Little Breezes watched her go. Then they played hide and seek until jolly, round, red Mr. Sun had climbed out of bed and was smiling down on the Green Meadows.

Pretty soon along came Peter Rabbit, lipperty-lipperty-lip.

"Hello, Peter Rabbit!" shouted the Merry Little Breezes. "Come play with us!"

"Can't," said Peter Rabbit. "I have to go find some tender young carrots for my breakfast," and away he hurried, lipperty-lipperty-lip.

In a few minutes Jimmy Skunk came in sight and he seemed to be almost hurrying along the Crooked Little Path down the hill. The Merry Little Breezes danced over to meet him.

"Hello, Jimmy Skunk!" they cried. "Come play with us!"

Jimmy Skunk shook his head. "Can't," said he. "I have to go look for some beetles for my breakfast," and off he went looking under every old stick and pulling over every stone not too big for his strength.

The Merry Little Breezes watched him for a few minutes and then raced over to the Laughing

Brook. There they found Billy Mink stealing softly down towards the Smiling Pool.

"Oh, Billy Mink, come play with us," begged the Merry Little Breezes. "Can't," said Billy Mink. "I have to catch a trout for Grandfather Mink's breakfast," and he crept on towards the Smiling Pool.

Just then along came Bumble the Bee. Now Bumble the Bee is a lazy fellow who always makes a great fuss, as if he was the busiest and most important fellow in the world.

"Good morning, Bumble," cried the Merry Little Breezes. "Come play with us!"

"Buzz, buzz, buzz," grumbled Bumble the Bee. "Can't, for I have to get a sack of honey," and off he hurried to the nearest dandelion.

Then the Merry Little Breezes hunted up Johnny Chuck. But Johnny Chuck was busy, too busy to play. Bobby Coon was asleep, for he had been out all night. Reddy Fox also was asleep. Striped Chipmunk was in such a hurry to fill the pockets in his cheeks that he could hardly stop to say good morning. Happy Jack Squirrel just flirted his big tail and rushed away as if he had many important things to attend to.

Finally the Merry Little Breezes gave it up and sat down among the buttercups and daisies to talk it over. Every one seemed to have something to do, every one but themselves. It was such a busy world that sunshiny morning! Pretty soon one of the Merry Little Breezes hopped up very suddenly and began the maddest little dance among the buttercups.

"As we haven't anything to do for ourselves let's do something for somebody else!" he shouted.

Up jumped all the Little Breezes, clapping their hands.

"Oh let's!" they shouted.

Way over across the Green Meadows they could see two long ears above the nodding daisies.

"There's Peter Rabbit," cried one. "Let's help him find those tender young carrots!"

No sooner proposed than off they all raced to see who could reach Peter first. Peter was sitting up very straight, looking this way and looking that way for some tender young carrots, but not one had he found, and his stomach was empty. The Merry Little Breezes stopped just long enough to tickle his long ears and pull his whiskers, then away they raced, scattering in all directions, to see who could first find a tender young carrot for Peter Rabbit. By and by when one of them did find a field of tender young carrots he rushed off, taking the smell of them with him to tickle the nose of Peter Rabbit.

Peter wriggled his nose, his funny little nose, very fast when it was tickled with the smell of tender young carrots, and the Merry Little Breeze laughed to see him.

"Come on, Peter Rabbit, for this is my busy day!" he cried.

Peter Rabbit didn't have to be invited twice. Away he went, lipperty-lipperty-lip, as fast as his long legs could take him after the Merry Little Breeze. And presently they came to the field of tender young carrots.

"Oh thank you, Merry Little Breeze!" cried Peter Rabbit, and straightway began to eat his breakfast.

Another Merry Little Breeze, slipping up the Crooked Little Path on the hill, spied the hind legs of a fat beetle sticking out from under a flat stone. At once the Little Breeze remembered Jimmy Skunk, who was hunting for beetles for his breakfast. Off rushed the Little Breeze in merry whirls that made the grasses sway and bend and the daisies nod.

When after a long, long hunt he found Jimmy Skunk, Jimmy was very much out of sorts. In fact Jimmy Skunk was positively cross. You see, he hadn't had any breakfast, for hunt as he would he couldn't find a single beetle.

When the Merry Little Breeze danced up behind Jimmy Skunk and, just in fun, rumpled up his black and white coat, Jimmy quite lost his temper. In fact he said some things not at all nice to the Merry Little Breeze. But the Merry Little Breeze just laughed. The more he laughed the crosser Jimmy Skunk grew, and the crosser Jimmy Skunk grew the more the Merry Little Breeze laughed. It was such a jolly laugh that pretty soon Jimmy Skunk began to grin a little sheepishly, then to really smile and finally to laugh outright in spite of his empty stomach. You see it is very hard, very hard indeed and very foolish, to remain cross when someone else is perfectly good natured.

Suddenly the Merry Little Breeze danced up to Jimmy Skunk and whispered in his right ear. Then he danced around and whispered in his left ear. Jimmy Skunk's eyes snapped and his mouth began to water.

"Where, Little Breeze, where?" he begged.

"Follow me," cried the Merry Little Breeze, racing off up the Crooked Little Path so fast that Jimmy Skunk lost his breath trying to keep up, for you know Jimmy Skunk seldom hurries.

When they came to the big flat stone Jimmy Skunk grasped it with both hands and pulled and pulled. Up came the stone so suddenly that Jimmy Skunk fell over flat on his back. When he had scrambled to his feet there were beetles and beetles, running in every direction to find a place to hide.

"Thank you, thank you, Little Breeze," shouted Jimmy Skunk as he started to catch beetles for his breakfast.

And the Little Breeze laughed happily as he danced away to join the other Merry Little Breezes on the Green Meadows. There he found them very, very busy, very busy indeed, so busy that they could hardly find time to nod to him. What do you think they were doing? They were toting *gold!* Yes, Sir, toting gold! And this is how it happened:

While the first Little Breeze was showing Peter Rabbit the field of tender young carrots, and while the second Little Breeze was leading Jimmy Skunk to the flat stone and the beetles, the other Merry Little Breezes had found Bumble the Bee. Now Bumble the Bee is a lazy fellow, though he pretends to be the busiest fellow in the world, and they found him grumbling as he buzzed with a great deal of fuss from one flower to another.

"What's the matter, Bumble?" cried the Merry Little Breezes.

"Matter enough," grumbled Bumble the Bee. "I've got to make a sack of honey, and as if that isn't enough, old Mother Nature has ordered me to carry a sack of gold from each flower I visit to the next flower I visit. If I don't I can get no honey. Buzz-buzz-buzz," grumbled Bumble the Bee.

The Merry Little Breezes looked at the million little flowers on the Green Meadows, each waiting a sack of gold to give and a sack of gold to receive. Then they looked at each other and shouted happily, for they too would now be able to cry "busy, busy, busy."

From flower to flower they hurried, each with a bag of gold over his shoulder. Wherever they left a bag they took a bag, and all the little flowers nodded happily to see the Merry Little Breezes at work.

Jolly, round, red Mr. Sun climbed higher and higher and higher in the blue sky, where he can look down and see all things, great and small. His smile was broader than ever as he watched the hurrying, scurrying Little Breezes working instead of playing. Yet after all it was a kind of play, for they danced from flower to flower and ran races across bare places where no flowers grew.

By and by the Merry Little Breezes met Peter Rabbit. Now Peter Rabbit had made a good breakfast of tender young carrots, so he felt very good, very good indeed.

"Hi!" shouted Peter Rabbit, "come play with me."

"Can't," cried the Merry Little Breezes all together, "we have work to do!"

Off they hurried, while Peter Rabbit stretched himself out full length in a sunny spot, for Peter Rabbit also is a lazy fellow.

Down the Crooked Little Path onto the Green Meadows came Jimmy Skunk.

"Ho!" shouted Jimmy Skunk as soon as he saw the Little Breezes, "come play with me."

"Can't," cried the Little Breezes, "for we are busy, busy, busy," and they laughed happily.

When they reached the Laughing Brook they found Billy Mink curled up in a round ball, fast asleep. It isn't often that Billy Mink is caught napping, but he had had a good breakfast of trout, he had found no one to play with and, as he never works and the day was so bright and warm, he had first looked for a place where he thought no one would find him and had then curled himself up to sleep.

One of the Little Breezes laid down the bag of gold he was carrying and creeping ever so softly over to Billy Mink began to tickle one of Billy's ears with a straw.

At first Billy Mink didn't open his eyes, but rubbed his ear with a little black hand. Finally he jumped to his feet wide awake and ready to fight whoever was bothering him. But all he saw was a laughing Little Breeze running away with a bag of gold on his back.

So all day long, till Old Mother West Wind came with her big bag to carry them to their home behind the Purple Hills, the Merry Little

Breezes hurried this way and that way over the Green Meadows. No wee flower was too tiny to give and receive its share of gold, and not one was overlooked by the Merry Little Breezes.

Old Mother Nature, who knows everything, heard of the busy day of the Merry Little Breezes. Nobody knows how she heard of it. Perhaps jolly, round, red Mr. Sun told her. Perhaps—but never mind. You can't fool old Mother Nature anyway and it's of no use to try.

So old Mother Nature visited the Green Meadows to see for herself, and when she found how the Merry Little Breezes had distributed the gold she was so pleased that straightway she announced to all the world that thenceforth and for all time the Merry Little Breezes of Old Mother West Wind should have charge of the distribution of the gold of the flowers on the Green Meadows, which they have to this day.

And since that day the Merry Little Breezes have been merrier than ever, for they have found that it is not nearly so much fun to play all the time, but that to work for some good in the world is the greatest fun of all.

So every year when the gold of the flowers, which some people do not know is gold at all but call pollen, is ready you will find the Merry Little Breezes of Old Mother West Wind very, very busy among the flowers on the Green Meadows. And this is the happiest time of all.

CHAPTER XIV

~

WHY HOOTY THE OWL DOES NOT PLAY ON THE GREEN MEADOWS

The Merry Little Breezes of Old Mother West Wind were having a good-night game of tag down on the Green Meadows. They were having *such* a jolly time while they waited for Old Mother West Wind and her big bag to take them to their home behind the Purple Hills. Jolly, round, red Mr. Sun had already put his night-cap on. Black shadows crept softly out from the Purple Hills onto the Green Meadows. The Merry Little Breezes grew sleepy, almost too sleepy to play, for Old Mother West Wind was very, very late.

Farther and farther and farther out onto the Green Meadows crept the black shadows. Suddenly one seemed to separate from the others. Softly, oh so softly, yet swiftly, it floated over towards the Merry Little Breezes. One of them happened to look up and saw it coming. It was the same Little Breeze who one time stayed out all night. When he looked up and saw this seeming shadow moving so swiftly he knew that it was no shadow at all.

"Here comes Hooty the Owl," cried the Little Breeze.

Then all the Merry Little Breezes stopped their game of tag to look at Hooty the Owl. It is seldom they have a chance to see him, for usually Hooty the Owl does not come out on the Green Meadows until after the Merry Little Breezes are snugly tucked in bed behind the Purple Hills.

"Perhaps Hooty the Owl will tell us why it is that he never comes out to play with us," said one of the Little Breezes.

But just as Hooty the Owl floated over to them up came Old Mother West Wind, and she was in a great hurry, for she was late, and she was tired. She had had a busy day, a very busy day indeed, hunting for a rain cloud which had gone astray. So now she just opened her big bag and tumbled all the Merry Little Breezes into it as fast as she could without giving them so much as a chance to say "Good evening" to Hooty the Owl. Then she took them off home behind the Purple Hills.

Of course the Merry Little Breezes were disappointed, very much disappointed. But they were also very sleepy, for they had played hard all day.

"Never mind," said one of them, drowsily, "to-morrow we'll ask Great-Grandfather Frog why it is that Hooty the Owl never comes out to play with us on the Green Meadows. He'll know."

The next morning Old Mother West Wind was late in coming down from the Purple Hills. When she finally did turn the Merry Little Breezes out of her big bag onto the Green Meadows jolly, round, red Mr. Sun was already quite high in the blue sky. The Merry Little Breezes waited just long enough to say "Good-by" to Old Mother West Wind, and then started a mad race to see who could reach the Smiling Pool first.

There they found Great-Grandfather Frog sitting on his big green lily pad as usual. He was very contented with the world, was Grandfather Frog, for fat green flies had been more foolish than usual that morning and already he had all that he could safely tuck inside his white and yellow waistcoat.

"Good morning, Grandfather Frog," shouted the Merry Little Breezes. "Will you tell us why it is that Hooty the Owl never comes out to play with us on the Green Meadows?"

"Chug-a-rum," said Great-Grandfather Frog, gruffly, "how should I know?"

You see, Grandfather Frog likes to be teased a little.

"Oh, but you do know, for you are so old and so very wise," cried the Merry Little Breezes all together.

Grandfather Frog smiled, for he likes to be thought very wise, and also he was feeling very good, very good indeed that morning.

"Chug-a-rum," said Grandfather Frog. "If you'll sit perfectly still I'll tell you what I know about Hooty the Owl. But remember, you must sit perfectly still, *per-fect-ly* still."

The Merry Little Breezes sighed, for it is the hardest thing in the world for them to keep perfectly still unless they are asleep. But they promised that they would, and when they had settled down, each one in the heart of a great white water lily, Grandfather Frog began:

"Once upon a time, when the world was young, Hooty the Owl's grandfather a thousand times removed used to fly about in daylight with the other birds. He was very big and very strong and very fierce, was Mr. Owl. He had great big claws and a hooked bill, just as Hooty the Owl has now, and he was afraid of nothing and nobody.

"Now when people are very big and very strong and afraid of nothing and nobody they are very apt to care for nothing and nobody but themselves. So it was with Mr. Owl. Whatever he saw that he wanted he took, no matter to whom it belonged, for there was no one to stop him.

"As I have already told you, Mr. Owl was very big and very strong and very fierce and he was a very great glutton. It took a great many little birds and little animals to satisfy his appetite. But he didn't stop there! No, Sir, he didn't stop there! He used to kill harmless little meadow people just for the fun of killing, and because he could. Every day he grew more savage. Finally no one smaller than himself dared stir on the Green Meadows when he was around. The little birds no longer sang. The Fieldmice children no longer played among the meadow grasses. Those were sad days, very sad days indeed on the Green Meadows," said Grandfather Frog, with a sigh.

"At last old Mother Nature came to visit the Green Meadows and she soon saw what a terrible state things were in. No one came to meet her, for you see no one dared to show himself for fear of fierce old Mr. Owl.

"Now I have told you that Mr. Owl was afraid of nothing and nobody, but this is not quite true, for he was afraid, very much afraid of old Mother Nature. When he saw her coming he was sitting on top of a tall dead stump and he at once tried to look very meek and very innocent.

"Old Mother Nature wasted no time. 'Where are all my little meadow people and why do they not come to give me greeting?' demanded old Mother Nature of Mr. Owl.

"Mr. Owl bowed very low. 'I'm sure I don't know. I think they must all be taking a nap,' said he.

"Now you can't fool old Mother Nature and it's of no use to try. No, Sir, you can't fool old Mother Nature. She just looked at Mr. Owl and she looked at the feathers and fur scattered about the foot of the dead stump. Mr. Owl stood first on one foot and then on the other. He tried to look old Mother Nature in the face, but he couldn't. You see, Mr. Owl had a guilty conscience and a guilty conscience never looks anyone straight in the face. He did wish that Mother Nature would say something, did Mr. Owl. But she didn't. She just looked and looked and looked and looked straight at Mr. Owl. The longer she looked the uneasier he got and the faster he shifted from one foot to the other. Finally he shifted so fast that he seemed to be dancing on top of the old stump.

"Gradually, a few at a time, the little meadow people crept out from their hiding places and formed a great circle around the old dead stump. With old Mother Nature there they felt sure that no harm could come to them. Then they began to laugh at the funny sight of fierce old Mr. Owl hopping from one foot to the other on top of the old dead stump. It was the first laugh on the Green Meadows for a long, long, long time.

"Of course Mr. Owl saw them laughing at him, but he could think of nothing but the sharp eyes of old Mother Nature boring straight through him, and he danced faster than ever. The faster he danced the funnier he looked, and the funnier he looked the harder the little meadow people laughed.

"Finally old Mother Nature slowly raised a hand and pointed a long forefinger at Mr. Owl. All the little meadow people stopped laughing to hear what she would say.

"'Mr. Owl,' she began, 'I know and you know why none of my little meadow people were here to give me greeting. And this shall be your punishment: From now on your eyes shall become so tender that they cannot stand the light of day, so that hereafter you shall fly about only after round, red Mr. Sun has gone to bed behind the Purple Hills. No more shall my little people who play on the Green Meadows all the day long have cause to fear you, for no more shall you see to do them harm.'

"When she ceased speaking all the little meadow people gave a great shout, for they knew that it would be even as Mother Nature had said. Then began such a frolic as the Green Meadows had not known for many a long day.

"But Mr. Owl flew slowly and with difficulty over to the darkest part of the deep wood, for the light hurt his eyes dreadfully and he could hardly see. And as he flew the little birds flew around him in a great cloud and plucked out his feathers and tormented him for he could not see to harm them."

Grandfather Frog paused and looked dreamily across the Smiling Pool. Suddenly he opened his big mouth and then closed it with a snap. One more foolish green fly had disappeared inside the white and yellow waistcoat.

"Chug-a-rum," said Grandfather Frog, "those were sad days, sad days indeed for Mr. Owl. He couldn't hunt for his meals by day, for the light blinded him. At night he could see but little in the darkness. So he got little to eat and he grew thinner and thinner and thinner until he was but a shadow of his former self. He was always hungry, was Mr. Owl, always hungry. No one was afraid of him now, for it was the easiest thing in the world to keep out of his way.

"At last old Mother Nature came again to visit the Green Meadows and the Green Forest. Far, far in the darkest part of the deep wood she found Mr. Owl. When she saw how very thin and how very, very miserable he was her heart was moved to pity, for old Mother Nature loves all her subjects, even the worst of them. All the fierceness was gone from Mr. Owl. He was so weak that he just sat huddled in the thickest part of the great pine. You see he had been able to catch very little to eat.

"'Mr. Owl,' said old Mother Nature gently, 'you now know something of the misery and the suffering which you have caused others, and I think you have been punished enough. No more may you fly abroad over the Green Meadows while the day is bright, for still is the fear of you in the hearts of all my little meadow people, but hereafter you shall not find it so difficult to get enough to eat. Your eyes shall grow big, bigger than the eyes of any other bird, so that you shall be able to see in the dusk and even in the dark. Your ears shall grow large, larger than the ears of any of the little forest or meadow people, so that you can hear the very least sound. Your feathers shall become as soft as down, so that when you fly none shall hear you.'

"And from that day it was even so. Mr. Owl's eyes grew big and bigger until he could see as well in the dusk as he used to see in the full light of day. His ears grew large and larger until his hearing became so keen that he could hear the least rustle, even at a long distance. And when he flew he made no sound, but floated like a great shadow.

"The little meadow people no longer feared him by day, but when the shadows began to creep out from the Purple Hills each night and they heard his voice 'Whoo-too-whoo-hoo-hoo' they felt all the old fear of him. If they were wise they did not stir, but if they were foolish and so much as shivered Mr. Owl was sure to hear them and silently pounce upon them.

"So once more Mr. Owl grew strong and fierce. But only at night had anyone cause to fear him, and then only the foolish and timid.

"And now you know," concluded Grandfather Frog, "why it is that Hooty the Owl never comes out to play with you on the Green Meadows, and why his eyes are so big and his ears so large."

"Thank you, thank you, Grandfather Frog!" cried the Merry Little Breezes, springing up from the white water lilies and stretching themselves. "We'll bring you the first foolish green fly we can find."

Then away they rushed to hunt for it.

CHAPTER XV

~

DANNY MEADOW MOUSE LEARNS TO LAUGH

Danny Meadow Mouse sat on his doorstep and sulked. The Merry Little Breezes of Old Mother West Wind ran past, one after another, and pointing their fingers at him cried:

> "Fie, Danny Meadow Mouse!
> Better go inside the house!
> Babies cry—oh my! oh my!
> You're a baby—go and cry!"

Pretty soon along the Lone Little Path came Peter Rabbit. Peter Rabbit looked at Danny Meadow

Mouse. Then he pointed a finger at him and said:

> "Cry, Danny, cry!
> Mammy'll whip you by and by!
> Then we'll all come 'round to see
> How big a baby you can be.
> Cry, Danny, cry!"

Danny Meadow Mouse began to snivel. He cried softly to himself as Peter Rabbit hopped off down the Lone Little Path. Soon along came Reddy Fox. He saw Danny Meadow Mouse sitting on his doorstep crying all by himself. Reddy Fox crept up behind a tall bunch of grass. Then suddenly he jumped out right in front of Danny Meadow Mouse.

"Boo!" cried Reddy Fox.

It frightened Danny Meadow Mouse. He jumped almost out of his skin, and ran into the house crying at the top of his voice.

"Ha, ha, ha," laughed Reddy Fox

"Danny, Danny, crying Dan
Boo-hoo-hooed and off he ran!"

Then Reddy Fox chased his tail all the way down the Lone Little Path onto the Green Meadows.

By and by Danny Meadow Mouse came out again and sat on his doorstep. He had stopped crying, but he looked very unhappy and cross and sulky. Hopping and skipping down the Lone Little Path came Striped Chipmunk.

"Come play with me," called Danny Meadow Mouse.

Striped Chipmunk kept right on hopping and skipping down the Lone Little Path.

"Don't want to," said Striped Chipmunk, sticking his tongue in his cheek.

"Cry-baby Danny
Never'll be a manny!
Run to mamma, Danny, dear,
And she will wipe away your tear!"

Striped Chipmunk hopped and skipped out of sight, and Danny Meadow Mouse began to cry again because Striped Chipmunk would not play with him.

It was true, dreadfully true! Danny Meadow Mouse *was* a cry-baby and no one wanted to play with him. If he stubbed his toe he cried. If Striped Chipmunk beat him in a race he cried. If the Merry Little Breezes pulled his whiskers just in fun he cried. It had come to such a pass that all the little meadow people delighted to tease him just to make him cry. Nowhere on all the Green Meadows was there such a cry-baby as Danny Meadow Mouse.

So Danny sat on his doorstep and cried because no one would play with him and he was lonely. The more he thought how lonely he was, the more he cried.

Presently along came old Mr. Toad. Now Mr. Toad looks very grumpy and out of sorts, but that is because you do not know old Mr. Toad. When he reached the house of Danny Meadow Mouse he stopped right in front of Danny. He put his right hand behind his right ear and listened. Then he put his left hand behind his left ear and listened some more. Finally he put both hands on his hips and began to laugh.

Now Mr. Toad's mouth is very big indeed, and when he opens it to laugh he opens it very wide indeed.

"Ha, ha, ha! Ha, ha, ha!" laughed Mr. Toad.

Danny Meadow Mouse cried harder than ever, and the harder he cried the harder old Mr. Toad laughed. By and by Danny Meadow Mouse stopped crying long enough to say to Mr. Toad:

"What are you laughing for, Mr. Toad?"

Mr. Toad stopped laughing long enough to reply:

"I'm laughing, Danny Meadow Mouse, because you are crying at me. What are you crying for?"

"I'm crying," said Danny Meadow Mouse, "because you are laughing at me." Then Danny began to cry again, and Mr. Toad began to laugh again.

"What's all this about?" demanded some one right behind them.

It was Jimmy Skunk.

"It's a new kind of game," said old Mr. Toad. "Danny Meadow Mouse is trying to see if he can cry longer than I can laugh."

Then old Mr. Toad once more opened his big mouth and began to laugh harder than ever. Jimmy Skunk looked at him for just a minute and he looked so funny that Jimmy Skunk began to laugh too.

Now a good honest laugh is like whooping cough—it is catching. The first thing Danny Meadow Mouse knew his tears would not come. It's a fact, Danny Meadow Mouse had run short of tears. The next thing he knew he wasn't crying at all—he was laughing. Yes, Sir, he actually was laughing. He tried to cry, but it was of no use at all; he just *had* to laugh.

The more he laughed the harder old Mr. Toad laughed. And the harder Mr. Toad laughed the funnier he looked. Pretty soon all three of them, Danny Meadow Mouse, old Mr. Toad and Jimmy

Skunk, were holding their sides and rolling over and over in the grass, they were laughing so hard.

By and by Mr. Toad stopped laughing.

"Dear me, dear me, this will never do!" said Mr. Toad. "I must get busy in my garden.

> "The little slugs, they creep and crawl
> And eat and eat from spring to fall
> They never stop to laugh nor cry,
> And really couldn't if they'd try.

So if you'll excuse me I'll hurry along to get them out of my garden."

Mr. Toad started down the Lone Little Path. After a few hops he paused and turned around.

"Danny Meadow Mouse," said old Mr. Toad, "an honest laugh is like sunshine; it brightens the whole world. Don't forget it."

Jimmy Skunk remembered that he had started out to find some beetles, so still chuckling he started for the Crooked Little Path up the hill. Danny Meadow Mouse, once more alone, sat down on his doorstep. His sides were sore, he had laughed so hard, and somehow the whole world had changed. The grass seemed greener than he had ever seen it before. The sunshine was brighter and the songs of the birds were sweeter. Altogether it was a very nice world, a very nice world indeed to live in. Somehow he felt as if he never wanted to cry again.

Pretty soon along came the Merry Little Breezes again, chasing butterflies. When they saw Danny Meadow Mouse sitting on his doorstep they pointed their fingers at him, just as before, and shouted:

"Fie, Danny Meadow Mouse!
Better go inside the house!
Babies cry—oh my! oh my!
You're a baby—go and cry!"

For just a little minute Danny Meadow Mouse wanted to cry. Then he remembered old Mr. Toad and instead began to laugh.

The Merry Little Breezes didn't know just what to make of it. They stopped chasing butterflies and crowded around Danny Meadow Mouse. They began to tease him. They pulled his whiskers and rumpled his hair. The more they teased the more Danny Meadow Mouse laughed.

When they found that Danny Meadow Mouse really wasn't going to cry, they stopped teasing and invited him to come play with them in the long meadow grass. Such a good frolic as they did have! When it was over Danny Meadow Mouse once more sat down on his doorstep to rest.

Hopping and skipping back up the Lone Little Path came Striped Chipmunk. When he saw Danny Meadow Mouse he stuck his tongue in his cheek and cried:

> "Cry-baby Danny
> Never'll be a manny!
> Run to mamma, Danny dear,
> And she will wipe away your tear!"

Instead of crying Danny Meadow Mouse began to laugh. Striped Chipmunk stopped and took his tongue out of his cheek. Then he began to laugh too.

"Do you want me to play with you?" asked Striped Chipmunk, suddenly.

Of course Danny did, and soon they were having the merriest kind of a game of hide and seek. Right in the midst of it Danny Meadow Mouse caught his left foot in a root and twisted his ankle. My, how it did hurt! In spite of himself tears did come into his eyes. But he winked them back and bravely began to laugh.

Striped Chipmunk helped him back to his doorstep and cut funny capers while Mother Meadow Mouse bound up the hurt foot, and all the time Danny Meadow Mouse laughed until pretty soon he forgot that his foot ached at all.

When Peter Rabbit came jumping along up the Lone Little Path he began to shout as soon as he saw Danny Meadow Mouse:

"Cry, Danny, cry!
    Mammy'll whip you by and by!
    Then we'll all come 'round to see
    How big a baby you can be.
    Cry, Danny, cry!"

But Danny didn't cry. My, no! He laughed instead. Peter Rabbit was so surprised that he stopped to see what had come over Danny Meadow Mouse. When he saw the bandaged foot and heard how Danny had twisted his ankle Peter Rabbit sat right down on the doorstep beside Danny Meadow Mouse and told him how sorry he was, for happy-go-lucky Peter Rabbit is very tender-hearted. Then he told Danny all about the wonderful things he had seen in his travels, and of all the scrapes he had gotten into.

When Peter Rabbit finally started off home Danny Meadow Mouse still sat on his doorstep. But no longer was he lonely. He watched Old Mother West Wind trying to gather her Merry Little Breezes into her big bag to take to their home behind the Purple Hills, and he laughed right out when he saw her catch the last mischievous Little Breeze and tumble him, heels over head, in with the others.

"Old Mr. Toad was right, just exactly right," thought Danny Meadow Mouse, as he rocked to and fro on his doorstep. "It *is* much better, oh very much better, to laugh than to cry."

And since that day when Danny Meadow Mouse learned to laugh, no one has had a chance to point a finger at him and call him a cry-baby. Instead every one has learned to love merry little Danny Meadow Mouse, and now they call him "Laughing Dan."

THE END

Other books by Thornton W. Burgess available as Dover reprints

The Adventures of Johnny Chuck (0-486-28353-4)

The Adventures of Mr. Mocker (0-486-48101-8)

The Adventures of Old Man Coyote (0-486-29646-6)

The Adventures of Old Mr. Toad (0-486-40385-8)

The Adventures of Paddy the Beaver (0-486-41305-5)

The Adventures of Peter Cottontail (0-486-26929-9)

The Adventures of Poor Mrs. Quack (0-486-27818-2)

The Adventures of Prickly Porky (0-486-29170-7)

The Adventures of Reddy Fox (0-486-26930-2)

The Adventures of Sammy Jay (0-486-44946-7)

The Adventures of Unc' Billy Possum (0-486-43031-6)

The Burgess Animal Book for Children (0-486-43745-0)

The Burgess Bird Book for Children (0-486-42840-0)

The Burgess Seashore Book for Children (0-486-44253-5)

Thornton Burgess Bedtime Stories (0-486-47916-1)

Whitefoot the Wood Mouse (0-486-44944-0)

(Log on to **www.doverpublications.com** for more information.)